D1713995

# When He Comes Back Around

## Love forced apart, a miscarried baby, now he's back...

A complete story, brought to you by best selling author Mary Peart.

When Jewel and Jordan were 15, they were high school sweethearts. Jewel was certain she had met the boy of her dreams, until he unexpectedly moved away to Europe and left her broken-hearted.

Fast forward into adulthood, and Jewel is happily content with how her life is going. That is, until she discovers Jordan has returned to take over his father's business, and is looking to reconnect with the love of his life.

Jewel wants this too, she really does.

But time changes things, and despite being as dashing as ever, Jordan has a lot of making up to do.

Will the two be able to reconnect lost love after all these years? Or will Jewel be left broken-hearted for a second time, with even worse consequences?

Find out in this exciting and passionate pregnancy romance by bestselling author Mary Peart of BWWM Club.

Suitable for over 18s only due to sex scenes so hot, you'll be wishing for your own star-crossed romance.

## Get Free Romance eBooks!

Hi there. As a special thank you for buying this book, for a limited time I want to send you some great ebooks completely **free of charge** directly to your email! You can get it by going to this page:

## www.saucyromancebooks.com/physical

You can see a the cover of these books on the next page:

**These ebooks are so exclusive you can't even buy them.**
When you download them I'll also send you updates when
new books like this are available.

Again, that link is:

## www.saucyromancebooks.com/physical

# Contents

# Chapter 1

"He's back!" Jewel stirred the cinnamon stick in her mug of black coffee and pretended not to hear what her friend had just said. It was mid afternoon break at the bookstore and Savannah had come over to have coffee as usual. "Are you listening to me, Jews?" she continued.

Jewel looked up and met her friend's eyes. "I know, and I heard you the first time." She said quietly. She had heard he was back because it had been all over the papers: 'Jordan McIntyre takes over from deceased father,' and then it had gone into details of the progress of the billion dollar company and how essential McIntyre and Company was in the small town. She had gazed at his picture in the paper that had done justice to his wildly streaked brown hair and his amazing emerald green eyes and the dimple in his strong chin. It had not shown his tall muscular frame or the whiteness of his teeth.

"Can we not talk about Jordan please, Savannah?" Jewel's large dark eyes pleaded with her friend's. They were missing one of the trios. Jaclyn had a showing of an apartment and had said that she was not sure she would make it. The three girls had been friends since high school and even when they had gone to different colleges they had still kept in touch. Savannah was a Junior high school teacher and Jewel had taken over the running of a very successful bookstore from her mother, who had gone to live in Florida with her new husband.

"You want to talk about how I left Jeremy's sorry ass?" Savannah asked her. Jewel looked at her friend in consideration, searching the perfectly made-up cocoa brown complexion and the elegantly combed shoulder length hair.

"You don't look the worse for wear." Jewel commented. "What did he do this time?"

"Caught him with his pants down, literally." Savannah told her. "He was screwing the next door neighbor and I came home early and caught them together... in my bed! I felt like burning my Egyptian cotton sheets but I remained sensible and told both of them to get the hell out of my apartment. I wanted to cut his cheap penis off but instead I had to be satisfied with cutting up his expensive Jordan sneakers."

"When did all of this happen?" Jewel asked laughing at her friend's expression.

"Over the weekend, but I didn't want to burden you with it considering," the rest was left unsaid but Jewel knew she was referring to Jordan being back.

"I am over him, Sav." Jewel said quietly.

"Girl, you don't need to go back there after all that happened." Savannah said sympathetically. "So now I am back on the market. Lord I hate starting over! Maybe that's why I put up with Jeremy's crap for so long."

"Sometimes it's better to stay alone than to go through all that." Jewel told her.

"Not all of us are as strong as you are honey. Sometimes a woman just needs a strong man to lean on and to relieve the stress with a little bit of sex, even if it is lousy sex."

"Settling is not my thing and you know it."

"You are looking for Mr. Perfect and he does not exist. You need to start settling for Mr. Available. Jordan was close to perfect and look where it got you." Savannah looked at her anxiously, afraid she had brought up painful memories, but Jewel shook her head.

"I have discovered that even perfection has its flaws."

\*\*\*\*\*

Jordan McIntyre sat around the massive old fashioned desk that had belonged to his father, and tried to get his bearings. He had been back in town for a week now and he had yet to get his head screwed on straight. He had not wanted to come back, mainly because of the strain between him and his parents, and he was not sure he wanted to see Jewel. He stared off into space as he thought how idealistic and stupid he had been to love her. He had thought that she loved him back, but had only been interested in his money.

He had felt like his heart was about to explode when he had been told by his parents that they had offered her two million dollars and she had jumped at the chance to take it. He had not been surprised by what his parents had done, but he had been heartbroken that she had proven them right all along.

They had met in high school because although his parents were so influential, they had wanted to show that they were a part of the community; that they not only employed locally, but that they also allowed their only son to mingle with the locals as well. They had shared several classes together. One morning she had raced into school because she had been running late and had careened into him, spilling both their books onto the floor.

"I am sorry," she had told him breathlessly, her large dark brown eyes meeting his green ones. She had been fifteen and he had been seventeen and as a senior he did not mingle with juniors; but she was different, with her oval face and coffee and cream colored complexion ,and long dark hair caught up in a ponytail.

They had started going out secretly. The first time they had kissed, underneath an oak tree on the path to her home, they knew they belonged together. He had been with several other girls at school, but the minute he touched her he knew he could not be with anyone else. He just needed a way to tell his parents about her. She had two strikes against her as far as they were concerned: she was black and she was not rich, so she did not belong.

"When are you going to tell them, Jordan?" she had asked him quietly, as they lay underneath their favorite tree in the cool spring afternoon. He had brought a blanket in his back pack and he had spread it out for them to lie on.

"Soon," he had told her briefly, pushing up her blouse to touch her small breasts with their dusky nipples. They had not gone all the way yet because she said she was not ready. He had respected her wishes, even though he was getting frustrated. "That's not good enough," she said pushing his hand away and pulling down her blouse.

"What do you want from me, Jews?" he asked her, resorting to the pet name he and her friends used for her.

"I want you to show me that I am not your dirty little secret." She had told him firmly.

He looked up sharply as he heard a discreet knock on the door. "They are ready for you now Mr. McIntyre," his father's secretary said to him.

"Thank you, I will be right there." He told her briefly, coming back to the present. The past had done him enough harm; he did not need to be rehashing it inside his head.

*****

Caroline McIntyre stared at her reflection in the large oval mirror in the large peach and cream bathroom. She had had a few nips and tucks done and frowned a little bit at the crinkles beside her eyes. She ran her fingers through her still full and glossy blonde hair, and reflected that for a woman of fifty seven years she looked ten years younger. It had taken a mountain of work and a personal trainer who did not let her slack off. It was because of that that she was toned and lean and in very good health. She was not like most of her friends: a cliché of going to bed with the trainer, and besides, hers was as gay as the night was long. She demanded respect and sleeping around with the hired help did not get you any. Servants talked and she was smart enough to realize that; her mother had been a helper too so she knew. She had married into wealth and she knew it was because of her good looks and the fact that she had not dropped her panties for James McIntyre when he had asked her to. She had been modest and had waited until he had put a ring on her finger. She had studied the etiquette and lifestyle of the rich and powerful like it was the Holy Grail, and adapted, until a lot of people thought she had been born into it.

Her husband had died of a heart attack and her son was back from Europe. It was then that she had realized that he had grown up, so unlike the gauche young man who had left four years ago. She had no doubt he would run the company in the best way possible. She just had to make sure he stayed away from that girl, or else all their efforts to keep them apart would have been for nothing!

*****

Jewel eased her tired feet out of her sensible working shoes and sat down heavily on the living room sofa, resting her head back and closing her eyes wearily. It had been very busy at the bookstore and she had been doing the books as well. Every time she had said she was going to employ someone else, she was constantly telling herself that the money could be put to proper use like purchasing some more computers for the students who frequently came in to do research and buy books.

Jordan was back! The thought came unbidden to her mind, and she felt herself shiver with the implication of it all. She had told Savannah that she was over him and had even convinced herself too, but she knew it was not true. They had left things undone and unsaid and she knew eventually they would have to see each other. He had been the love of her life, and even though she had tried to date after the horrible experience; she had found that it had made no sense.

She got up and padded into the small kitchen to make herself a bowl of plain soup. It was getting chilly out and she had felt the October cold biting into her jacket as soon as she stepped out of the car.

She had been foolish to believe that she would have been accepted into his family. They were the most influential family in the community and employed thousands of people in one business or another. He had told her that his family would accept her because he loved her, so how ow could they not love her as well? Jordan had said teasingly. He had introduced her to them the night before the senior prom and she had seen the look on their faces. He had known with a sinking heart that their time together had been limited. She had told him and he had brushed it off. It had been confirmed when his mother had taken her aside with the pretext of showing her around the mansion they lived in.

"I admire your courage and fortitude for thinking that you can become a member of the McIntyre family," she had said pleasantly enough. "Jordan has stars in his eyes right now, and you are different so that's a novelty to him. You will never be accepted here my dear, so I am advising you to get out before you get your heart broken."

She had been subdued and quiet for the rest of the evening and no amount of coaxing from him would get her to reveal what was wrong with her.

His mother had been right, but she had not gotten out without a broken heart; he had not only broken her heart but had left her to pick up the pieces of a broken life.

*****

"Is this going to be our lives from now on?" Jaclyn demanded as she poured herself a second glass of wine and curled her feet underneath her on the bed. It was Sunday and the three girls had gotten together at Jaclyn's house to have dinner and hang out. "We need to get our groove back on and go out to the clubs and meet men. We are not even thirty years old, yet here we are having dinner and drinking wine like we have passed the prime of our lives!"

"I am mourning the passing of boyfriend number three," Savannah said dramatically flopping down on the soft eiderdown pillows on her friend's bed. "I think three weeks is the necessary mourning period."

"Did you just make that up?" Jewel asked her mildly. The three women turned heads wherever they went. Jewel was the shortest of them but the most beautiful, with a serene expression on her oval face. After Jordan had left, she had finally decide to get her life back. She had cut off her shoulder length hair, now cropped close to her face, highlighting her large dark brown eyes and drawing attention to her full lips. She had dimples in both cheeks and her smile lit up her face in an extraordinary manner. Both Savannah and Jaclyn had shoulder length hair and tall willowy bodies, but Jewel had gently swaying hips and a generous bosom.

"I am sure I saw it somewhere," Savannah said with a grin.

"Honey, that guy was a no good from the get go," Jaclyn said placing her empty wine glass on the side table. "There is nothing more pathetic than a brother who refuse to get a damn job! And you were encouraging him, having him stay in the apartment that you paid for, and buying him clothes and crap! He should have been gone as soon as he said hello."

"He was trying to find himself," Savannah protested.

"Of course he was, and he was using your money to do it." Jaclyn said dryly. "It's no wonder sisters are turning to white guys these days. Speaking of which," she turned to Jewel who were looking at them in amusement. "Have you seen him?" she demanded.

They all knew who she was referring to, and even though they were her best friends she hated discussing Jordan with them. "No, I haven't," she told her friend forcing herself to act calm.

"I saw his plastic looking mother driving past as I was about to go inside a house I was showing. She looked as if she owned the world." Jaclyn said in distaste. "That woman has forgotten entirely where she came from."

Her friends had been there for her when the whole thing had gone down and had held her while she cried her eyes out and booted her out of bed when she had thought her life was over so she owed them a lot. "That's all in the past now so we don't have to keep bringing it up."

"Is it?" Savannah looked at her shrewdly. "I have my doubts about that."

*****

"Honey are you sure you are okay?" Sylvia Blake, formerly Walsh asked her in concern. She had gone home a little tipsy from the wine and was lying down for a little bit when her phone rang.

"Mom, I am sure." Jewel said stifling a sigh.

"I don't know why he had to come back when you had been doing so well," she fretted.

"This happens to be his home mom, and I am still doing well." Jewel reminded her.

"If you want me to come back honey and spend some time with you, I will. George is forever playing golf anyway," she could hear the pout in her mother's voice.

"No mom, I am fine. I really don't need you to hold my hand."

"Honey, I am just being a mother. You don't have to sound so abrupt." Sylvia retorted.

"I know, and I am sorry, but I am getting tired of the subject of Jordan right now, I just want to forget he exists."

"That's going to be very difficult considering that he had been so much a part of your life and you both shared so much together." Sylvia said wisely.

"I am still going to try." She said firmly, turning the conversation to her mother's husband. "How is he coping with hurting his back in the car accident.?"

"He is doing better than both of us and planning to go back into the office in the next two weeks." Sylvia told her. George Blake owned a car lot that was doing very well; well enough that her mother could afford to stay home.

"Tell him hello for me. I will talk to you later."

"Ok, honey. Remember, you can always call your mother if you need anything."

*****

"Jordan, darling, I wish you would talk to me about what's going on," Caroline complained. They were sitting around the large dining table in the living room having dinner. They had to practically shout to be heard. He had suggested that they had dinner in the smaller dining room, but she had refused, saying that it was not appropriate and they needed to keep up appearances where the servants were concerned.

"If there was anything to tell, trust me mother, you would be the first to know." He told her briefly, cutting into his beef wellington. He hated the place and thought it was too large and pretentious, especially for two people. He had a good mind to sell it. His mother would have a fit because she liked being lady of the manor too much. "Profits are up and the shipping line is doing very well. I have been trying to streamline the pharmaceutical part of it and seeing if there was some way to make the drugs more affordable for the locals."

"Darling, you know how I hate to discuss business, especially when we are eating. I was talking about your social life." She said looking at him calculatingly. "That sweet Penelope Barrington has been asking about you. She has landed a job in the big law firm in town, not the ideal career choice for a woman like her but very commendable."
"I don't need you to choose a companion for me mother. I am perfectly capable of doing so myself." He lifted his wine glass and looked at her coolly, his green eyes inscrutable. He knew

what she was doing and he had no intention of being a part of it.

"Of course not darling," She protested, placing the napkin she had been dabbing her lips with, on the beautiful lace table cloth. "I just think it's time you settled down, that's all."

"I am not ready yet," he told her briefly. "If you'll excuse me?" and without waiting for her to answer he left the table feeling as if he was going to suffocate.

He had his own suite of rooms and he quickly made his way there, going into his living room and pouring himself a glass of scotch. He hated the taste of it, but whenever he was with his mother he always felt like he needed a strong drink.

He stared into the glass broodingly, his brow furrowed. He had dated quite a bit when he had been in Europe trying to forget but it had not worked. He had gone to bed with a number of women, but he always ended up feeling the bitter taste of regret the next morning. He had finally given up and realized that it was no use, she was under his skin and there was no getting her out. With a bitter laugh he tossed the liquid down and grimaced at the after taste that he had never acquired. He had not seen her since he had been back but he knew exactly where she was; the bookstore her mother used to run. Why hadn't she taken the money and put it to good use? What had she done with it? He wondered bitterly. Was she seeing someone else and if so, were they making love the way he had made love to her? Was he stroking her nipples the way she liked it when he had done it to her? He had been the first for her, and he remembered how he had captured her tears as he pushed past her barrier. He closed his eyes as he remembered how she had wrapped around him and fitted like a glove. and when he had started moving inside her, how she had clung to him and arched her body against his. Her hands were wrapped around his neck and her fingers buried in his hair. He had wiped her down gently with a napkin and she had cried out as he explored inside her with his fingers. He had made love to her again, kissing her over and over again!

He threw the glass into the fireplace, his body shaking! She was not going to do it to him again! He would not allow it.

# Chapter 2

"Here you are, and thank you for coming," Jewel said with a smile, as she handed the package to the elderly Mrs. Hodges. She was the last customer for the day and Jewel wanted to lock up and get going. She had a session at the gym and she needed to work out some issues. She had not slept well the night before and the disturbing thoughts kept inching inside her mind.

She had just gone over to lock the door behind the elderly woman when she saw him standing there. Her heart stood still and she was transported back to four years ago. He looked like a male model, only more muscular and toned. He had acquired a deep tan which looked excellent against his brown hair streaked liberally with blonde. His dark green eyes held hers and for a moment she felt weak; but only for a moment. "Jordan," she forced a polite smile to her lips as she stood just inside the doorway, not giving him the impression that she wanted him inside. "What are you doing here?"

"Aren't you going to let me in?" he asked in an amused drawl, shoving his hands into the pockets of his dark blue dress pants.

"I was just leaving," she said standing her ground.

"This will only take a minute," he stood his ground as well, his eyes locking with hers.

She hesitated a little bit and then, biting back a sigh, opened the door wider to let him in making sure to stay as far away from him as possible.

"You made some changes." He said looking around the place and noticing the reading corner and the internet section.

"Yes," she said briefly, wanting him to leave. "What do you want, Jordan?"

"Is that anyway to talk to your ex- man?" he asked lifting a thick brown brow.

"Emphasis on ex," she told him in a wintry voice, not believing that he was being so callous. "You are wasting both our times Jordan, and I have somewhere to be. I am sure being the big shot CEO you are right now you probably have some business meeting to attend."

"You have become quite the bitch, haven't you?" his voice was steely and he was coming closer to her. She had to get him to leave.

"Stop!" she cried holding up one hand and stopping him in his tracks. "I can't bear to see you, be in the same room with you. I wished you had not come back, but I can't stop that. What I can prevent however, is you coming near me. I want you to stay away from me Jordan, and I mean it."

His eyes had turned a turbulent green and she knew from past experience that it was when he was most furious. She did not care; she just wanted him to leave. "You got it," he told her coldly. Taking another look around the store he said something confusing. "I am surprised with all that money, that you have not done more." With that he wrenched open the door and left the store. Jewel quickly locked the door and pulled down the shade, and only then did she allow her emotions to get the better of her. With a tortured sob she slid down on the floor and allowed the tears to fall.

*****

Aerobics session had just started when she got to the gym. Both Savannah and Jaclyn were already in line and they gave her a cross look as she hastily got behind them to start doing the knee lifts. It was a gym that was patronized by most of the women in the community. Jewel had once seen Jordan's mother there with her personal trainer, but she had not been back.

After a hectic half an hour of jumping and jogging, the friends went to choose appropriate sized weights to tone their arms. "We thought you weren't coming," Jaclyn said mildly, lifting her arms and bringing them back down.

"Jordan stopped by," she told them casually. She had washed her face in cold water and patted it dry and peered closely in the mirror to see if it was evident that she had had a crying jog before putting on her gym clothes and leaving.

"Are you kidding me?" Savannah who had been sitting on one of the benches and working her arms stopped to look at her friend. "I hope you told him where to go put his head."

"What did he want?" Jaclyn asked looking at her friend curiously.

"I did not give him a chance to tell me. I told him to leave and he said something very strange to me. He said that he would have thought I would have done more with the money I got." Jewel dabbed the perspiration from her brow with the towel she had around her neck. She had been puzzling about the remark ever since she had had time to think about what he said.

"What does that mean?" Savannah asked.

"Beats me." Jewel said with a shrug.

"White people. Who knows what they mean when they say something cryptic," Savannah said with a shake of her head. "That's why I only date brothers; at least you know what the hell they are talking about."
Both her friends stared at her as if they were just seeing her for the first time. "What?"

"I can't believe you just said that. You are supposed to know better, being a teacher." Jaclyn told her in disgust. "Men are men honey, no matter what color the package is. As long as they have penises, the thinking is the same."

"But the length is different," Savannah said with a leer. "Remember the saying: 'Once you go black you can never go back.' "

"I beg to differ," Jewel said quietly. "Jordan had a very decent length, and he is very white."

Her friends stared at her in shock. She never usually indulged in that kind of conversation and certainly never about Jordan. "I am just saying." She said with a nonchalant grin.

The two girls burst out laughing so loudly that the others in the room turned to stare at them. The tension of the previous discussion had been effectively dispelled.

*****

Jordan paced. He had not gone to his mother's side of the house but had entered from his part, hoping that she had not seen when he had driven in. He did not know what had possessed him to go to the bookstore, but he had felt as if something was pulling him there. It had been the same when he had tried to stay away from her when he had first discovered how he felt about her. It had been so strong that even when he was at home he would feel the pull of his body towards hers. It was not just physical, it was mental as well. Even in spite of what he had been told that she had done, he still wanted to see her. It had been a huge mistake, he thought, his hands clenched at his sides. She was even more beautiful than ever; and her hair! She had cut it and instead of detracting from her beauty, it had somehow managed to enhance it. He closed his eyes and remembered how she looked in her green pants and black silk shirt. She was still petite, and he remembered how he had always teased her about barely reaching to his shoulders. Her breasts had filled out and he had seen the generous curves against the material. He had wanted to touch her, to feel her against him and to drink from her lips. His body shuddered as he felt the powerful arousal invaded his body. He rested his head against the coolness of the wall and with a deep groan realized that it was starting all over again... if it had ever stopped!

*****

Jewel looked up as the doorbell tinkled, the smile that had been curving her lips disappearing as she realized who it was. Caroline McIntyre; the woman who had made her life a living hell because she had deigned to love her son.

It was a few minutes after four and the crowd had somewhat dwindled down . Jewel was glad she had chosen to wear her new outfit, a rose red pants suit and gold accessories glinting at her ears and her wrists. Not that she had anything to prove to her.

"Such a quaint little place," the woman said sweetly, pulling off her expensive suede gloves. She had a fur wrap which she pulled off, and for a minute Jewel thought she was about to hand it to her to hang up. "I see you have fixed it up a bit." Her green eyes so much like his, met hers.

"How may I help you?" she asked the woman politely, trying not to grit her teeth.

"Help me?" her laughter tinkled out and she came further inside the room. Jewel wondered what she had done to be getting visits from the McIntyre's; Jordan last week and now his mother. "I doubt you can my dear. I am just here to make sure you stay away from my son."

Jewel's dark brown eyes flashed. She had been so afraid of this woman before, but now she knew better. "Oh, you don't have to tell me that. Why don't you tell your son to stay away from me?" She saw the expression on the woman's face and almost smiled in triumph. "He did not tell you he came around here last week almost boring his way inside the store? I had to tell him to leave in no uncertain terms."

The red spots on her cheeks made her look unattractive. Score one for me! Jewel thought grimly. How dared she think she could run her life like she did before!

Without a word she turned on her expensive stiletto heels and headed for the door. "Nice to see you. Do come back again," she called out as the woman pulled the door open. She hesitated and turned her coiffed blonde head to look at the younger woman and Jewel held her gaze steadily, Caroline was the first to turn away before the door closed behind her.

With a sigh and a smile Jewel realized that her hands were not trembling and her heart was not racing. She was no longer intimidated by the powerful McIntyre family.

*****

Caroline was furious! That little chit! Who did she think she was? Nobody talked to her like that! She had gone back home and was sitting in the green house breathing in the pungent aromas of the many variety of flowers planted there. She prided herself on her green thumb and even though she had employed the very best to take care of her plants, she herself pottered around in the soil as much as the gardener did. She had come home and changed out of her clothes and put on faded denim overalls and told the maids not to disturb her. Jordan had been to see her, but he never said anything to her. He had changed so much since he had returned, more taciturn than usual and very secretive. He also seemed very grown up and hard, like he was ailing from something or someone, and no amount of throwing different eligible women at him was working, she thought grimly. She had kept a small intimate dinner party and had invited Karen Schneider, the daughter of a judge and a debutante who looked like she could have been a model. A Jordan had called from the office to tell her that he would not be home for dinner.

She had broken them up four years ago and offered money to get rid of her. The girl had torn up the check in front of her and had left, saying she did not need anything from them. She had shown her son the check stub with the girl's name on it and had convinced him not to call her. It was after he left that she discovered that the girl had been pregnant and had lost the child as she tumbled down the stairs to the library where she had been doing some studying. She had kept all of that from her son and with a spark of fear she knew that she could never let him know what she had done or she would lose him forever!

\*\*\*\*\*

Jewel went into the bathroom to renew her make-up and re-polish her lips with the nude color lip gloss. Her friends had dragged her out to this new and trendy club, saying it was a Saturday night and girls were going to have fun. So far the fun had not started for her, and it was almost ten o'clock. Both Savannah and Jaclyn were chatting up two brothers who claimed they owned their own businesses, but Jewel had stayed at the bar, toying with her fruit cocktail. She had gone home from the store, showered, and dressed in tight black jeans and a figure hugging black sweater with a plunging neckline, and high heeled black boots. She glanced over to where her friends were drinking and laughing with the two men and wished she could just let go of everything and enjoy herself.

"You are way too beautiful to be by yourself," a male voice said beside her.

Jewel closed her eyes and turned towards him. He was tall and bad headed with dark skin and a white smile. "Does that line really work on anyone?" she asked him with a cool look.

"It's not a line, it's actually the truth. What's a beautiful woman like you doing at the bar all by herself?"

"Obviously, because I want to be alone." She told him pointedly, turning back to her drink and wishing he would go away.

"My name is Terrence," he waited, hoping that she would tell him her name. "May I buy you a drink?" he continued when she did not answer.

"No thank you, I am already drinking." She turned back to him. "Look, I am sure you are a nice guy and all that, but I am not interested. I just want to enjoy my drink and be left alone."

"So are you a lesbian or what?" he asked with a sneer. The nice guy had disappeared with just a few words.

"No, she just wants you to get the hell away from her!" a soft menacing voice said behind them. The man jumped off the stool and scurried away.

"I don't need you to protect me," she told him, stiffly refusing to turn and look at him. He took the stool the man had just deserted. "Don't you?" he asked her mildly. "A gin and tonic please, Roger," he told the bartender.

"Yes Mr. McIntyre, sir."

"Are you following me?" she finally turned to look at him and wished she hadn't. He was wearing a gray sweater and denims and his hair was falling on his forehead, He looked and smelled like health and sex all rolled into one.

"No, this just happens to be the latest acquisition of McIntyre and Company." He told her grimly. "I am definitely not following you."

"I wished I had known before, I would have gone someplace else." Jewel responded coolly, meaning it.

"When did you change from the sweet beautiful girl I know, to this hard bitter woman I don't recognize?" his question was asked quietly but his tone was bewildered.

"I learned from the best," she sent him a cool sidelong glance leaving him in no doubt as to where she had learned her lesson. He captured her eyes with his and Jewel felt as if she was drowning in their depths. She tore her eyes away from his and looked towards her friends and realized that the men had taken their leaves and they were giving her their full attention.

"I see you have your bodyguards as usual," he commented cynically looking in their direction. Even in high school when they had found out about her and Jordan, they had been against the relationship, telling her he was too 'white,' and worse, he was too rich and nothing good will come of it. They had been so right.

"Please, excuse me," she made as if to slide off the stool but he reached out and took her arm, stopping her.
"Dance with me." He said suddenly.

"What?" she looked at him startled.

"One dance," he said urgently.

"No," she told him firmly.

"Afraid I might stir up feelings inside that had been dormant for a while?" he taunted her, with a grim smile that did not quite reach her eyes.

"Don't flatter yourself," she told him coolly. "Those feelings are long dead." She used her eyes to look at him from head to the expensive leather boots he was wearing. "I moved on years ago." With that she wrenched her arm away from him and forced herself to walk towards her friends slowly; deliberately swaying her hips for his benefit.

"Quite a performance," Jaclyn said with a grin. "Savannah and I were about to come over but we saw you dealt with it all on your own."

"Let's go," she said bleakly, shrugging into her black leather fall jacket and heading for the door.

*****

She had just taken off her boots and was just about to go to the bathroom when she heard a knock on the door. "I told you girls to try and sleep it off-" she stopped in mid sentence as she looked into the peephole and realized that it was Jordan. She rested her head against the door and contemplated whether or not she should let him in.

"I know you are in there Jewel and I am not leaving until I talk to you."

She sighed and opened the door, barring him from coming in. "What is it Jordan?" she asked him wearily. Now that she had taken off her boots she had to tilt her head to look up at him.

"We left things unfinished all those years ago, and I am wondering what you feel like now that you are older. Who is screwing you now Jewel?" his tone was silky and she smelled the liquor on his breath.

"Are you drunk?"

"With two glasses of gin and tonic?" he scoffed. "Of course not. Who is he?"

"That's none of your business," She started to close the door in his face and he braced it back and came inside. "I spent so many years trying to forget your delectable little body and how you feel under me and the taste of your lips. I went to bed with women of all type just to erase you from my mind, but the image remained. I am back in town and I zero in on you, when I can have any woman I want. What have you done to me?" the last part was said in a pitiable whisper, and to her horror she realized that she wanted him to kiss her! He saw what she was trying to hide and with a deep groan he pulled her into his arms. Jewel fought it and she even put up a token resistance but as soon as his lips met hers she knew she had lost the battle! She opened her mouth underneath his and he crushed her to him, deepening the kiss, his tongue delving inside her mouth as his arms tightened around her waist. He half lifted her up against him and braced her back against the closed door, kissing her hungrily. Jewel clenched her fists into his sweater and kissed him back with all the desperation she was experiencing. The first time he had kissed her had been after a game against a rival team. He had been the quarter back and he had come away from the rest of the guys. They had slipped around the side of the building and he had lifted her up against him and devoured her lips, leaving her weak and wanting more. This was like that time, only more intense, and if she did not stop him she was going to beg him to take her. She tore her mouth away from him and forced the desire racing through her body to stop. "I have had better. Your time in Europe has taught you a thing or two, so thank you for demonstrating that. Now, would you please leave?" she held the door open for him and forced herself to meet his eyes. What she saw there made her want to flee, but she held her ground.

"Liar," he jeered softly and without another word, he left. Jewel closed and locked the door behind him, her hands shaking badly. She did not know what she was going to do if he did not stay away from her!

# Chapter 3

"Darling, you are not eating. Is something the matter?" Caroline asked him in concern. They were sitting in the dining room having their weekly dinner. She had asked the chef to prepare his special Peking duck and wild rice and strawberry truffles for dessert.

"It doesn't add up," he reasoned mostly to himself, toying with the baked potato on his plate. "Aside from the inclusion of computers and a reading corner the shop looks the same and her apartment is tiny with furniture that looks like she had had them for years. Why didn't she use the money to expand, or buy herself a fancy apartment or a fancy car? She drives an old Corolla."

The only thing his mother heard was that he had been to her apartment! What was he doing there? "You went to her place?" she had lost her appetite and she felt as if she was going to pass out! What if he found out? What if he asked her?

"Honey, she probably invested it someplace." She said desperately. She was trying to get him off track. "You know her. Was she the type to spend money on clothes and all that?"

He shook his head and his brow cleared. "You are right, she was not into that."

"There you go!" Caroline almost sagged with relief. "That explains everything."

"It does," he said quietly, pushing away the plate with the food barely touched and making as if he was ready to leave the table.

"You haven't eaten anything." Caroline protested, trying to stop him from leaving. She barely got to see him because he spent most of his time at the office. When he did come home, he did not use the main entrance but went around the side to go into his suite.

"I am not hungry, and please tell Stefan that his cooking is superb as usual." He said with a little smile.

"You loved her very much, didn't you?" she asked him as he pushed his chair backwards.

He went still and his green eyes looked at her. "I think I still do." He said with a small smile. "I keep trying to find reasons why I should not and reminding myself about what she did, but it is not working. I am running out of ways to stop thinking of her."

Caroline felt her heart twist inside her! What had she done? Because of her bias she had messed up two peoples' lives and there was no way of fixing it.

"I am sorry darling," she said softly, he would never know how much, she thought sadly.

"So am I mother." With that he left the table and went to his suite, leaving her looking after him with tears in her eyes.

*****

"I wish you would come with us." Savannah said plaintively. They were at her house after work having a glass of wine before they went on a double date with the guys they had met that night at the club.
"And do what?" Jewel asked dryly. "Sit there watching you make moon eyes at Tyler and Blake?" It had been a week since Jordan had pushed his way inside her apartment and kissed her and she had not seen him since. She told herself she was glad, but she was still remembering his mouth on hers. She had not told her friends because she knew exactly

what they would say. This was her friend's second date and they were going to dinner at the fancy restaurant uptown.

"We could ask Tyler or Blake to hook you up with one of their friends from the office." Both men were corporate lawyers and things seemed to be going well.

"No thank you," Jewel said firmly. "I have things to do like sort out some shipments for the bookstore, and I have not cleaned the apartment in weeks."

"So you will be spending a Saturday night cleaning the apartment?" Jaclyn asked in disgust.

"And doing paperwork," Jewel reminded her with a grin.

"When did you become a retiree?" Savannah asked.

"I am just doing stuff I cannot afford to have others do for me. What's wrong with that?" Jewel protested.

"Everything." Jaclyn said throwing up her hands in the air dramatically. They had decided to stop by to see if they could get her to change her mind and come with them. She had on a slinky black dress that left her arms and back bare, and extremely high red heels. Savannah was wearing red leather pants and a clinging purple blouse. They both looked beautiful and well groomed and ready for a night on the town. "You are young and beautiful and you are wasting away in your apartment."

Jewel laughed! She could not help it. "You make it sound like I am suffering from a terminal illness."

"You might as well be," Jaclyn grumbled. "Okay Sav, it's time to hit the road; our dates will be waiting."

"Have fun you two," Jewel told them and meant it.

"We will and definitely, I am planning to test drive Blake's penis tonight." Savannah said with a grin. "From the bulge in his pants I would say he has potential."

"You are impossible," Jewel said shaking her head.

"I am holding on to mine for a little while longer." Jaclyn said loftily.

"Oh please!" Savannah said with a wave of her hand. "I need to get laid!"

Jewel saw them to the door and closed and locked it behind them. She had told them the truth and besides, she wanted to be alone. She tackled the laundry and while that was going on she cleaned out her closet. It was coming to winter and she needed to get her summer and fall clothes in a container to make room for her winter clothes.

She had just taken a shower and pulled on an old T-shirt over her damp skin when she heard the knock on the door. Her heart skidded inside her chest and she knew without looking through the peephole that it was Jordan. She could not let him in, if she did she was going to give in to her feelings.

The knocking continued and with a frustrated sound she went to look at the peephole. It was him, and his hair was disheveled as if he had run his fingers through it countless times.

She pulled the door open but stood there, blocking his path. His eyes were bloodshot as if he had not gotten any sleep for days, and he had a day's growth of hair on his strong jaw. "What is it, Jordan?"

"I drove around in the neighborhood and told myself that I should go home." He told her with a harsh laugh, bracing his hands on the door frame as if to steady himself. "I am not sleeping and I am not eating. Guess what I am doing?"

"I have no idea," she told him coolly, stifling the instinct to close her arms around him.

"Of course you don't," he said briefly. "I want to come inside Jews," he resorted to using her nickname and she felt herself weaken.

"No," she said trying to be firm. "I have things to do,"

"So do I," he pushed his way past her and stood in the center of the small living room.

Jewel closed and locked the door resignedly. She folded her arms across her chest and just remembered she was not wearing any bra.

"What is it about you?" he asked her softly, coming to stand in front of her. She forced herself to remain where she was. "I thought I was over you and I could come back here and see you without being affected. I spent the time in Europe thinking that I was cured and it took me getting back here to find out that I am far from being over you. What is this hold you have over me?" his hand lifted and cupped her cheek. Jewel felt the trembling starting and even if she wanted to move, she couldn't, she was rooted to the spot. "You are in my blood and under my skin, Lord help me," the last part was said like a broken prayer, a cry for help as he brought his head down and captured her mouth with his!

Even when they were teenagers their feelings for each other had often spiraled out of control. One touch and they would be fighting not to lunge at each other. Their love had become a powder keg and they had had to physically stay away from each other in order to maintain some sort of control. It had become more intense, if that was possible, and Jordan felt as if he wanted to eat her alive, to devour her whole. He picked her up and carried her towards the well worn sofa. He knelt before her, tearing his mouth away from hers, his turbulent green eyes sweeping her face. He pulled the shirt over her head and stared at her full and unfettered breasts with their dusky brown nipples, and with a tortured groan he took one inside his mouth, sucking on it in pure desperation. Jewel sobbed out loudly. As his hand went between her legs, she opened them for him. His mouth left her nipples and went down to her flat stomach until her reached her pubic area, where he licked her through the sheer material of her white lace panties. He had introduced her to the joy of oral sex the second time they had made love. They had been in a secluded part of the wooded area behind his house and he had gone down on his knees and started tonguing her. She had resisted at first, but when his tongue touched her, she had exploded and cried out his name desperately. It was the same thing now; as he pulled her panties down she was impatient for his mouth to take her.

"Shh," he told her hoarsely as she started to make little whimpering sounds. He brought his head down, his tongue went inside her and she cried out, her hands clenched into fists. He lifted her legs high above his head and used his tongue to thrust inside her, his teeth grazing her mound. She was almost delirious with need! He tortured her with his tongue, only stopping when he discovered she was on the verge of having an orgasm. He stood up and undressed hastily and stood there looking down at her with his penis in his hand. He was big! The first time she had seen it she had shied away thinking that he was going to hurt her very much but he had spoken softly to her, telling her that he would never hurt her. The thought entered her head to tell him to use protection, but the words could not come out of her mouth! He knelt before her and took her hand, placing it on his rigid penis. "Put it inside you," he told her tightly. She eased it inside her and he grasped her underneath her arms and brought her down on him. She was tight! His eyes narrowed as he looked at her. She had not been with anyone in a long time. "You lied," he gritted as he moved up inside her. "You almost destroyed me with your lie." He told her brokenly, holding her close and moving inside her. She closed around him and his thrust became urgent, gripping her body against his. She moved with him and clung to him, burying her face into his shoulder as he thrust up and into her. Jewel dug her nails into his shoulders and lifted her head to look at him. His hair was on his forehead and his green eyes were dark and turbulent with passion. He took her mouth with his as he felt the pressure building up inside his testicles. They came together and he captured her cries, his body convulsing against hers, his heart hammering inside his chest. He had tried to find this with someone else, anyone else, and it had not even come close. He wanted it back!

Jewel drifted firmly back to earth. She felt humiliation and anger wash over her. He had come over and she had not hesitated to drop her panties for him like before! This man and his family had caused her so much misery that for years she could not recover. She had gone through a miscarriage and lost their child and he had been half way around the world. His mother had told her that he did not want to hear anything from her as he was seeing someone else, he was practically engaged. He was still inside her and she tried to move but he held on to her. "No," he told her huskily. "I want you to stay."

"Tough!" it was very hard to make her voice sound cold when she was still sitting on his semi hard penis, but oh she tried! "I want you to leave right now."

"And if I don't?" His voice had gone soft and inflexible and Jewel almost grind her teeth in frustration.

"Okay fine! Yes, I am still attracted to you. How could I not be? You are very experienced and a very attractive man, not to mention very wealthy. What woman would not want to go to bed with you ?" she asked him scathingly.

He let her go and she got off him hastily, praying that he would not reach for her again. She desperately searched for her shirt and pulled it on, not bothering to look for her underwear.

He stood up slowly and stood there completely naked, looking at her. Jewel avoided looking at him but even though she was not looking at him directly, she could see the bronze hair on his chest that spread down to his genitals and his muscular build. He was magnificent and he made her weak.

"What happened to you?" he asked her softly. "Why are you so angry with me? You were the one who did not want me. You were the one who said that you had only been experimenting with a white guy, and now you are placing everything on me." He started putting on his clothes while she looked at him, puzzled. "I am going Jewel, but if you think this is over then you are a fool." He took one look at her before he left: at her spiked hair, her swollen lips and her breasts that had fed him so hungrily outlined against the shirt. He knew he could never stop loving her, and if possible it had grown to epic proportions. He left and closed the door quietly behind him.

Jewel locked the door and rested her head against the door. She was in deep trouble, she thought, feeling the tears starting!

*****

"We need to talk!" he said grimly as he pushed the door open and stepped inside the store. She had not seen him since the night they made love almost a week ago. She had spent the nights and most of the days reliving the incredible experience of being with him and had hid it from her friends in the process.

She had been on the verge of closing the store when he came in. He looked so handsome and so angry that she felt a shiver run up and down her spine. "No, we don't." she told him.

He locked the door and turned the sign from open to close.

"Who do you think you are?" Jewel asked him, her eyes flashing.

"The man who got you pregnant four years ago," he said trying to contain his anger and his hurt. He watched as she stepped back, her eyes wide. "Your friend Jaclyn gave me quite an earful and called me all sorts of names for not standing up to my responsibilities. Why wasn't I told that you were carrying my child Jewel? How could you keep something like that from me?"

"You left me!" she blazed at him, the anger bursting from her. "You left me without a contact number and with only your parents who told me you wanted nothing to do with me. I went through two months of pregnancy and a horrible miscarriage and you weren't there. You were jet setting your way through Europe."

Jewel saw the look of pain and disbelief on his face as he stood there looking at her.

"You thought I knew and ignored it?" he asked her quietly, his shoulders slumping in acute weariness. "You know me better than that. How could you think that of me?"

"Because I gave your mother a letter to send to you, and she said you told her that you wanted nothing to with me and a baby you are not even sure is yours." She told him angrily.

"My mother said that?" He was past being angry now. When Jaclyn had bumped into him in the restaurant a few nights ago she had lit into him like a flame that had been set off. He had been out with a friend of his because he had been trying to get a break from thinking about her. He sat there staring at her as she spilled the information about Jewel being pregnant.

"Just leave me alone Jordan. It's in the past and we have both moved on." She told him wearily, rubbing a hand at the back of her neck.

"You think this is over between us?" he gave a short bark of laughter, which had her looking up at him. "We are never going to be over. Stop lying to yourself, and to me!" He had come over and gripped her arms, forcing her up against him. "I can't stay away from you and I am tired of trying. I am so tired." He whispered resting his head against her forehead. "You were carrying my child inside you and I would have done anything to be with you. How could you not know that?" His breath fanned her face and she felt the desire starting. She wanted to hold him and tell him how much she had called his name and how she had cried for him. "What was it?"

"It was too early to tell," she murmured.

"I want another chance." He told her suddenly, putting her a little way from him. "I want us to have another child together."

Jewel felt the pounding of her heart and she almost said yes, until she came to her senses. "Are you out of your mind?" She tried to pull away from him, the whole awful experience flooding into her mind! The pain and despair of losing both him and their child almost at the same time! The amount of time it took to pick up the pieces of her life together. "I went through hell and back!" She practically screamed at him. "I was sick for the entire time I was carrying our child and if it was not for my mom and my friends, I would not have made it. I cried myself to sleep at nights wanting you, needing you to be there with me, and when I slipped and fell from those stairs at the library I thought I was going to die. I wanted to die when the doctor told me that I had lost my baby. I could not function for years...so don't come and ask me to do it again. I am not a fool for you anymore."

Every word she had said to him felt as if she had been driving a nail inside his heart and he wanted to go somewhere and die. She was right! He had no business telling her that he wanted a child from her after what she had been through. He was not there, and it did not matter that he had not known about it; it did not negate the fact that he had been missing in action!

"You are right," his tone was quiet and defeated. "I was not there for you and even though I had no idea of what was going on, the fact is I was not around and you will never know how much I regret that and how much I am suffering because of it." He bent his head and before she knew what he was about, he captured her lips with his, the movement tender and slow and searching. Jewel sagged against him, curling her hands into his cashmere sweater as his tongue touched hers. He released her mouth slowly and stepped back, his breathing irregular, his hands clenched at his sides as he fought for control. "I can't stay away Jewel. Whatever I have to do to make it up to you, I will do so." He turned to walk away. "How do you know you are not pregnant now?" the question was left up in the air as he opened the door and left.

# Chapter 4

"Darling, you are still here? I thought you would have been at the office by now." Caroline pulled her silk robe closer to her body as she made her way downstairs from her suite of her rooms. It was a little after nine and she had been at a dinner party until late last night.

"I am here because I need to talk to you." Jordan was barely holding on to his anger. "Have a seat, mother."

"This sounds serious," she said trying to keep her tone light.

"It is," He was already dressed for the office in a dark blue business suit and a light blue shirt and red tie but he had called his secretary and told her that he was running a bit late. "You and dad did not tell me that Jewel was carrying my child." It was not posed as a question. Caroline felt the increase in her heartbeat.

"We were trying to protect you, darling," she said swiftly trying to climb out of the pit she had dug herself into. "We were not sure the child would have been yours."

"Stop!" he gritted out, pacing in front of where she was sitting. "I was the only man for her and I have a feeling that I have been the only man for her. She was carrying my child, your grandchild and you did not think you could look past the ridiculous bias you have against her and let me know that I was going to be a father! What else did you lie about, mother? The two million dollars you claimed that she accepted; it was not true was it?"

She remained quiet for so long that Jordan realized with horror that all she and his father had told him about Jewel were all lies. The letter, the money everything! No wonder she could not bear to even look at him and he had made it worse by blaming her for something she had not done. How could she ever forgive him?

"You are going to fix it, mother," his voice had gone dangerously calm. "I don't care how you do it but you are going to fix it with her so that I will somehow be worthy of her love again. If you don't," he paused and raked her with his green gaze causing the fear to rise inside her. "If you don't, you will have lost a son and any future grandchildren. I love her and always will and that is never going to change, because if it's not her, then it's no one." With that he spun on his heels and left her sitting there, shivering in her thin silk robe in the large opulent living room.

*****

Jordan sat inside his car with the engine running. He had driven to the end of the driveway because he could not bear to be in the same vicinity as his mother. He had wanted to strangle her! She and his father had manipulated his life for so many years. He should have known her better than to think she would take money from them. She had never been impressed by his wealth and had always cut him down to size whenever he behaved as if he was better than anyone else. "Money does not make a person, Jordan." She had told him quietly one day, while they were sitting under their favorite tree. "It's what's inside that person that defines who they really are."

He had failed her and he did not deserve her back He rested his head against the steering wheel and felt the weight of despair on his shoulders. Their son or daughter would have been almost four years old now, he thought bleakly. How was he going to make her see past all the hurt and pain his parents, and inadvertently, he had caused her? How did he begin to tell her how sorry he was for not believing in her?

He gunned the engine and made his way to the office building of McIntyre and Company, staring up at the towering glass structure with his name in big white letters. So much wealth and so little happiness! He had been born into it and had never known what it felt like to want for anything in his life, except now, when he wanted the only thing he desired and ever had!

*****

Jewel smiled and gave the girl the book to continue reading to the children as she went to tend to several customers. It was Friday and it was usually busy, but this morning it was as if she had not even found the time to take a coffee break. She had her usual meeting with her friends later and was looking forward to just sitting down and unwinding.

She was in the middle of helping a customer choose an appropriate book for a child's birthday when the bell tingled. She looked up to see Jordan's mother standing just inside the doorway, staring around uncertainly.

www.SaucyRomanceBooks.com/RomanceBooks

With a supreme effort of being friendly, she excused herself from the customer and came over to her. "I do not have time to trade words with you today," she told the woman forcing herself to be polite. She did not look like her usual immaculate self but looked as if she had just left the house in a hurry and forgotten to put on make-up.

"I need to talk to you urgently." She said quietly, her expression looking like one on the brink of crying.

With a brief hesitation, Jewel beckoned to one of the high school girls to help her out and indicated that Caroline come with her to her little office. She waited on her to begin.

"Jordan is mad at me," she said with a short laugh. Still Jewel remained silent. The woman was twisting the straps of her designer bag in her hands as if the movement somehow made her feel better. "I did some very foolish things and now he is threatening never to speak to me again."
"I am sure he will come around, after all you are his mother," Jewel said politely.

"It has to do with you!" she said looking at the cool and beautiful girl in front of her and hated that she was in this position. "I did it all because I wanted to protect him,"

"From big bad me?" Jewel asked raising a tapered dark brow.

"I come from a very poor background and I thought –"

"You thought he should do better than me." Jewel finished the sentence. "Mrs. McIntyre, you should know better than anyone else that it matters not where you come from but where you end up and I am not talking about having lots of money. As long as you are happy with yourself and where you are, it does not matter if you have a cent. You and your husband thought you could choose for your son, and ended up destroying something wonderful. Jordan and I loved each other very much. The difference in our backgrounds did not matter because when we were with each other, everything faded away. I am so sorry you felt you had to change that."

The woman stared at the cool confident girl in front of her and realized that she was not the same person she had been before. She had grown up.

"He wants your forgiveness, and so do I." Caroline said stiffly.

"And in time I will be able to forgive both of you," Jewel told her coolly. "I lost my child Mrs. McIntyre, and you still have yours, consider yourself fortunate." She stood up, indicating that the meeting was at an end. Caroline felt the fear clutching her heart again.

"What should I tell Jordan?" her voice sounded desperate.

Jewel looked at her in surprise. "Tell him you spoke to me, or you can tell him whatever you want to. I am sure you are smart enough to come up with something."

The woman stood there staring at her and realized that the girl had more class in her little finger than she had in her whole body. She had spent the number of years she had been married to Jordan's father trying to learn how to be classy and had the feeling that she had failed drastically. Now standing in front of this cool and extremely beautiful girl, she definitely knew that she had.

"Thank you for hearing me out." She said quietly.
Jewel nodded briefly and followed her out.

She watched her closed the door behind her and it was only then that she let out a sigh. She was no longer the screwed up, bewildered girl she had been before!

*****

She was pregnant! Jewel stared at the stick, aghast. It had been three weeks since she had been with Jordan, and a week since his mother had come to see her. He had not called her or been back to see her. She had told herself she was happy, but she was aching to see him. She wanted to be with him and it was causing her sleepless nights. She had started feeling that something was wrong when she realized that her period had not come at the allotted time. She had chalked it down to the stress of Jordan coming back and her reaction to seeing him. She had been queasy in the mornings, even when she brushed her teeth.

Apart from the initial reaction of dismay, she realized that she wanted the child. When she had found out that she was pregnant the first time, even though he had left, she had been over the moon, thinking that at least she would have a part of him inside her and with her at all times. When she had had the miscarriage she had felt as if a huge part of her life had gone.

She hugged herself around the waist and sat down on the bathroom floor. She would have to tell her friends and her mother, and she knew what they were going to say. She had not told them that she had been with Jordan but had kept it to herself. It was too special for her to have them raking him over the coals for what they had done that night. But first she would have to tell Jordan, because even though she had no intention of starting back up where they had left off, he had a right to know. She had seen what not knowing about the first pregnancy had done to him. He never knew.

It was Sunday morning and she had decided to stay in bed and rest a little bit; she was feeling especially drained. She dialed his number and he answered on the second ring.

"I wanted to call you but I did not know what to say to you." He paused and she could hear the humility in his voice. "I can't believe I doubted you Jewel, and for that I cannot face you right now."

"I am afraid you will have to," she told him wryly. "I think I am pregnant."

The silence on the other end was profound. "I am coming over," he told her briefly hanging up the phone.

He was there in twenty minutes, giving Jewel just enough time to straighten up and take a shower, putting on a pair of old sweat pants and a black T-shirt.

The wind had tousled his hair and the gold in it shone in the dim light of the apartment. He had on a green sweater that rivaled the color of his eyes and was wearing faded denims. She had left the door open and he came straight in, his eyes going over her face.

He did not touch her and for that she was grateful. He sat beside her on the sofa and looked at her enquiringly. "Are you sure?" he asked her quietly. Ever since she had told him, he had been trying to restrain himself from flying high.

"I peed on two sticks and all the signs point to it, so I am sure." She said with a nod.

"You want me to make an appointment for the doctor?" he asked her. He wanted to take her into his arms and cried out in joy.

"I already did. Tomorrow at two o'clock. I just have to get someone to mind the store."

"I'll pick you up." He said immediately.

"Thanks," she told him.

He sat there looking at his hands clasped between his legs. "I don't expect you to forgive me or my parents for what happened. My mother told me that she spoke to you and what you said and I don't blame you." He stared in front of him, a bleak expression on his face. "I cannot forgive her, not right now, but I am hoping that one day we can go back to where we were before all this."

"We cannot go back Jordan, and going through all of that killed something inside me." He felt as if his heart was breaking into a million tiny pieces. "When I look at you I am always reminded that you were not there when I most needed you, and I cannot get past that, not right now. I loved you so much and when you left I wanted to die. I don't want to lose control over myself like that again. I am sorry."

"For what?" he asked her bitterly. "You have nothing to be sorry for. I screwed up and I cannot even blame my parents too much. I knew you, they didn't. I let them influence me into thinking the worse of you." He took a deep breath and then stood up. "I will be there tomorrow to pick you up, and thanks for including me in this Jewel. I promise I will not let you go through this by yourself."

She followed him to the door. He stopped just as she was about to close the door and hauled her into his arms, taking her lips in a kiss so hungry and desperate that Jewel felt herself responding in kind. He held her against his shuddering body as he thrust his tongue inside her mouth. With a hoarse cry he pushed her back inside and closed the door. He braced her back against it and fumbled for his erection, before pulling down her loose pants. He entered her forcefully, his control disappearing as he thrust inside her, his hands gripping her hips.

Jewel clung to him and moved against him with a desperation that matched his own!

*****

He picked her up from the store at a quarter to two. She had gotten one of her mother's friends to mind the store for her without going into details as to why she needed her help. He looked at her briefly as he came out and opened the door for her to get in, and then went back around to the driver's seat, pulling the white corvette from the curb. "How are you?" he asked her.

"I am fine; just a little bit queasy," she told him. After he had left last night she had been unable to sleep, feeling him inside her and his mouth on hers.

"I am sorry for that." He told her quietly.

"It comes with the territory." She told him with a little smile.

"Do you want my baby?" he asked her suddenly, giving her a brief look.

"What?' she looked at him startled wondering where the question had come from.

"After all we put you through, I was wondering if you wanted to have anything to do with the McIntyre name." his hand had tightened on the steering wheel.

"I will love my baby no matter what name it has, Jordan." She said softly.

"Somehow that does not make me feel any better." He said with a brief laugh.

"I did not say it to make you feel better or worse. I just said it."

"I know."

They continued the rest of the way in silence. They were ushered right in to see Dr. Livingstone, a fairly young female doctor who knew the McIntyre's very well, but who didn't?

She asked the questions and was told of the miscarriage several years ago after which she did the examination. "You are indeed pregnant, Jewel." She said with a smile. "Congratulations," she said to both of them. "I am going to give you something for the queasiness and some vitamins to help your body get accustomed to the child growing inside you. I want you to make an appointment to see me in the next month and a half."

"Thank you, doctor," Jordan spoke for the first time. "Will the –" he cleared his throat. "The miscarriage she had before will it affect the child growing inside her now?"

"No," the doctor told him. "She has been sufficiently healed for her to carry this baby to full term."

He took her hand as they left the doctor's office and went to the car. It was almost three thirty and she wanted to get back to the store. "You are carrying my child. I can't tell you how I feel," he turned towards her in the car, his hand resting on the steering wheel and the other near to her on her seat. "I want to be a part of my child's life in every way possible."

"You will be." She assured him. "I just cannot promise more than that right now Jordan, please understand."

"I am trying to," he told her before turning back to start up the car. "I just cannot deal with it right now. I want to be able to take you in my arms and go to my place and make love to you all day and talk about our child, but I cannot and it kills me that I can't even do that." He slammed his hand against the wheel, causing her to jump. "Don't be afraid of me, please don't! That's something I would never forgive myself for,"

She reached out and touched his face, seeing the look of torture there and felt her heart constrict. She never wanted to cause him pain, but there was something inside her that could not forget the horror she had been through. She needed to deal with that aspect first of all. "I would never be afraid of you." She told him softly, resting her palm against the roughness of his strong jaw. "You never gave me a reason to."

He placed his hand against hers and closed his eyes. Then with a gentle movement he removed her hand and drove out of the lot.

He dropped her off at the store and told her that he would call her later. "How about dinner?" he asked her quietly.

She was just about to say no when she saw the hopeful look on his face. "Okay, that sounds fine."

"Good," he nodded, a smile lighting up his handsome face as he drove away.

*****

"Can't you be happy for me?" She had finally told her friends everything. It had been three days since she had been to the doctor and had had dinner with Jordan at a restaurant of his choice. She had had to forego the rest of the meal because her stomach had been acting up. He had been so gentle with her that she had wanted to cry.

"You could have told us you were seeing him again." Jaclyn told her in an accusatory tone. They were at her apartment when she had called and told them that she had something to tell them.

"He came back to confront me after you reamed him out in that restaurant." Jewel told her with a little smile.

"Damn straight I did!" Jaclyn said, folding her long legs underneath her on the bed. "To his credit, he had never heard that you had been pregnant let alone had a miscarriage. The poor man looked as if I had ripped his freaking heart out!"

"What I don't get is how that crow of a mother could do something like that to her own son," Savannah asked, as she propped herself on the pillows against the headboard.

"I guess she thought she was protecting her son." Jewel offered.

"From whom?" Jaclyn asked dryly. "Now he knows who he needs protecting from."

# Chapter 5

"I want you to come to the house with me and I would like you to spend the night." Jordan's voice was quiet, a little short from pleading. She was four months pregnant now and the doctor had assured them that the baby was healthy. She had told her mother and she had asked her if she wanted her to come and be with her.

"No, mom I am fine. Jordan is here and Jaclyn and Savannah are getting on my nerves with their coddling." She told her mother.

"So where do you stand with each other?" she asked.

"We are just seeing each other. He takes me to every doctor's appointment and buys every fruit and vegetable imaginable for me to eat healthy, but that is it right now. I am not ready for anything more." Jewel said.

"I am sure he wants more, honey." Her mother had said gently.

"I can't give him more right now."

"No," she told him, her tone decisive.

"I know it's painful for you to come to my place Jewel, but I need to be with you," he said, trying not to sound exasperated. He needed to give her time and he had been trying to do so. He had finally told his mother and she had been inquiring about her, wondering if Jewel would forgive her before the baby was born.

"So be with me at my apartment." She was at the bookstore and had been serving a customer when he called. She had glanced outside and discovered that it had started snowing again. She had spent Christmas with her friends and the night with him. He had wanted her to spend it over at his place but she had refused. He had come over, making love to her until the morning and holding her against him while they slept.

"How long are you going to keep punishing me for, Jewel?" he asked her quietly. She handed the package to the lady with a smile and sat behind the cash register.

"I am not punishing you Jordan, but you know how I feel about coming over there." She told him.

"Would it help if I get myself an apartment?" he asked her suddenly.

"I would never ask you to do that," she told him hastily.

"Damn it Jewel! At least meet me halfway here." He said his voice rife with frustration.

"Okay Jordan, you can pick me up later." She told him with a sigh.

"Will you be spending the night?" he asked, his voice hopeful.

"Don't push it, Jordan." She warned him.

"I am not letting you go Jewel," he told her. She had a feeling he was not just talking about tonight.

"I am beginning to realize that." She told him dryly.

She replaced the receiver, her expression thoughtful. She still loved him, that had never and would never change, but she was being cautious. She had been through too much to just forget about it like that. She could see that he was trying but she was not ready to go all the way yet.

"Excuse me, do you have this title?" a petite blonde passed her a paper with the name of a book written on it.

Jewel read the title and looked up at her with a smile. "It so happens that we do." She indicated for her to follow her.

*****

Jordan sat in the boardroom and listened to the various reports. McIntyre and Company was a very diversified company and was involved in technology, pharmaceuticals, real estate and even shipping. He had discovered that his father had even bought several hairdressing salons which belonged to a certain lady by the name of Sally. He had dug a little deeper and had also found out that his so called stellar father, who did not tolerate anyone with the skin color darker than his, had been seeing this Sally, (who was as dark as a bar of chocolate) for years before his death. McIntyre still hold the title on the hairdressing salons even though her name was on it.

He had gone to visit her one afternoon to find out just how involved his father had been.

"Would you like some coffee?" the woman had asked him politely, her nervousness showing in the way she clasped her hands together. She was an attractive woman with shoulder length black hair and large dark brown eyes.

"No thank you," he had told her.

"I suppose you want to find out the nature of the relationship between your father and I before his death?" she sat down on the deep couch opposite to him.

"I already know you were his mistress Ms. Catheters, but what I want to know is why?" he had told her bluntly. "You are not exactly my father's type."

She smiled a little bit and looked down at her clasped hands. "I used to do your mother's hair. He came by one afternoon to pick her up and we sort of connected. At first he wanted to know how lucrative the business was and how much money could be made. You know your father," she told him briefly.

"I am afraid I do."

"Then it turned into something else. I knew about his prejudice towards people of color and even though he tried to hide it, it always showed." She caught his eyes. "I fell in love with him in spite of myself and I was even pregnant from him at one point." She looked away towards the far corner of the room.

"What happened?" Jordan leaned forward, but he was afraid he already knew the answer.

"He made me get rid of it," she bit down on her lip to stop it from trembling and Jordan felt every ounce of respect he had had for his father drain away. "He said it would not do for him to have a colored child and he was such a respectable man in town."

"And yet you stayed with him" Jordan's voice was grim.

"I don't expect you to understand," she had tears in her eyes and somehow she reminded him of Jewel, his Jewel. "I love him and did not want to lose him so I did what he asked and he showered me with gifts. That was when he bought the chain of salons for me, maybe to compensate for what he made me do."

"Was it worth it?"

"I will never be able to have another child now and he is dead. I have nothing of his to remind me of him, so the answer is no. If I had been a stronger woman I would have told him no and damn the consequences."

"You were up against the most powerful man in the town so I doubt you would have won." Jordan reassured her.

Sally looked at him gratefully. "You are nothing like him." she said with a soft smile.

"I should hope not." Jordan said firmly. "The color of a person's skin had never meant anything to me, only to my parents. The only woman I have ever loved is African American and has no money."

"He told me about that." Sally stared at him. "He also told me there was no way he was going to allow his only child to marry a 'negro'; forgetting that he was sleeping with one every night." She shook her head in disbelief. "He told me I was the exception."

"And you believed him?" Jordan asked watching her face. It was a lucky thing he was dead or there would have been some serious confrontations.

"Of course not, but I played along. The sad and pathetic thing is that I still love him and I would spend my nights spinning the fantasy that he would discover he could not live without me and he would come and be with me." She said sadly.

"My father never really loved anyone that much," Jordan told her dryly. "If it's any consolation he never really loved my mother either."

He gave her the title to the businesses and told her it was all hers.

"I wish you all the best, you and your young lady," she told him as he made towards the door. "She is very fortunate to have someone like you."

"I am the fortunate one," he told her briefly before leaving.

*****

"What would you like to eat?" he asked her as they were in the car going to his place. She had told him that she was too tired to go and sit in a restaurant. She just wanted to stretch her feet out and relax.

"You are going to cook?" she asked him, turning her head to look at him. He looked so handsome in his dark blue cashmere sweater over his light blue shirt and red tie and even though he had tried to tame his hair, there was still tendrils drifting onto his forehead that the wind had tousled.

"I could order take out. The chef has probably turned in for the night, or I could cook macaroni and cheese."

"You don't cook, Jordan," she reminded him with a laugh remembering him telling her that he had tried to cook an omelet and had almost burnt the place down.

"You are right, so take out it is." He told her with a smile.

He felt her hesitation as soon as he turned the car into the circular driveway. The place was massive and the house sat on several acres of land that led up to a small hill where they had sneaked there to be with each other. One time he had sneaked her inside the house and into his bedroom and they had made love on his bed two times.

"It's different now." He told her quietly. February had dumped some snow on the grounds but the place looked immaculately and she could see the greenhouse which was his mother's pride and joy in the far corner. She also knew that there was a huge pear shaped swimming pool, a tennis court and a basket ball court and a large cottage that was supposed to be the helpers' quarters.

"I know," she told him briefly as she walked with him towards his suite.

His bedroom and the sitting area had been redecorated and looked masculine but tasteful at the same time, with muted browns and faded red. They went into the living room where there was a fire burning in the large fireplace.

He ordered Chinese food and they were having it in the dining room when there was a discreet knock on the door. He stood up with a frown wondering why one of the servants would be bothering him at this time of the night.

He opened the door to discover to his consternation that it was his mother. Ever since he had discovered about her part in what he and Jewel had been through, he had been barely civil with her. "Not a good time, mother," he told her coolly.

"I know darling I just wanted to say hi to Jewel and to tell her how happy I am for you and her." Caroline said in a chastened voice. She had seen them walking across the grounds and just wanted to say something to the girl who meant so much to her son.

"Not now-"Jordan started to say but Jewel interrupted him.

"It's okay Jordan." She had come up behind him without him noticing. "Would you like to eat with us, Mrs. McIntyre?"

She stared at the girl and how gracious she was and nodded. "Thank you." She came in and noticed how Jordan reached for Jewel's hand as if to protect her.

They sat down and Jordan shared a plate for his mother. "I understand you are already four months along," she said hesitantly, not sure what to say.

"Yes I am. I have stopped feeling so queasy." She said smiling politely.

She realized that Jordan was not saying a word, probably waiting for her to make one wrong move so he could tell her to go.

"When I was pregnant with Jordan I ate like a horse and nothing upset me." She said with a laugh, looking at her son who did not even look at her. He was looking at Jewel instead and Caroline realized now more than ever, how much he loved her, and the extent of what she had done to both of them.

"I will leave you two to finish your dinner." She pushed back her chair and got ready to leave.

"No stay, please. Jordan and I don't mind." Jewel looked towards him for confirmation but he avoided her eyes.

"That's okay Jewel, another time perhaps." She said sadly and made for the door.

Jewel sent a furious stare towards Jordan and went after the woman. "I am sorry for Jordan's behavior." She got to her as she reached the end of the hallway.

"I understand why he is like that. I did a terrible thing and he is not able to forgive me yet." She paused with her hand on the beautiful curved banister. "I just hope he will come around so that I will be a part of my grandchild's life."

"I am sure he will," Jewel told her, feeling the anger towards her starting to drain away.

"Thanks." She smiled briefly and went back to her suite.

*****

"Save it!" he said between his teeth as soon as she came back into the room. He was clearing the table and heading towards the kitchen.

"Save what? The fact that you were very rude to your mother?" she asked him angrily following him into the large ultra modern kitchen.

"So you are suddenly on her side now?" he asked her cynically, dumping the plates in the sink.

"I am not on anyone's side Jordan, but you could at least be civil."

"I can't!" he cried out turning his back on her. "She was part of destroying the most important part of my life. Now I am trying desperately to get it back, and I feel as if I am failing."

His body was rigid. Jewel stood there for a moment and then she went up to him, wrapping her hands around his waist. "You have not lost me Jordan, I am still here." She told him resting her head against his back.

He braced his hands against the counter. "It's not the same Jewel. I want back what we had before, and because of what happened I have to be satisfied with what you give me."

"Please turn around," she pleaded.

He did so immediately and looked at her; the oval face that he knew so well, the curling of her lashes and the finely arched brow, the little mole at the side of her lips that he thought was so damn sexy, and those lips!

"We are together right now, and it's better than not being with each other at all. We have made a child together, we are getting there. You just have to be patient." She told him gently. He pulled her into his arms. "I am trying," he whispered against her mouth. "But it's so hard." He took her lips with his and lifting her, he took her inside the bedroom where he undressed her slowly and used his mouth on her to show her how much he was trying.

*****

"I dumped Tyler yesterday," Jaclyn said abruptly stretching her legs out on the lounge chair.

"Girl I thought it was going somewhere good." Jewel said in concern. They were at Savannah's apartment this time, and instead of sipping wine they were drinking hot chocolate and eating cookies that Savannah had made. It was two weeks since she had been to Jordan's place and spoken to his mother. She had been back a few times and spent the night there on Monday. She had told him she was going over to Savannah's place and she would see him tomorrow, being Saturday. She was starting to show and he wanted to take her shopping for baby clothes, but she was not ready yet.

"She is too picky," Savannah said with a shake of her head as she plopped back on the bed. "He told her that he wanted her to meet his parents and she told him she did not want to see him again."

"You dumped him because he wanted you to meet his parents?" Jewel stared at her friend in surprise.

"I am not ready for that kind of commitment." Jaclyn said with a shrug of her slim shoulders. "I am just in it for a good time, and he is boxing me into a corner trying to force my hand."

"The man is devastated and has been calling my phone and asking me what he did wrong." She stared at her friend in disgust. "You need to talk to him."

"I don't need to do anything!" she said crossly. "He will get over me soon enough."

"Why are you so afraid of commitment?" Jewel asked her softly.

"Look who is talking!" Jaclyn said with a sharp laugh, staring at her. "Here you are, getting bigger by the month with Jordan's child and practically over at his place with him all the time and yet you refuse to go and live with him. I bet the guy is dying to ask you to marry him."

"You know my reasons," Jewel said stiffly.

"Yes, and you have since discovered that those reasons are false. The man never stopped loving you and cannot bear to be away from you for a second. You need to put him out of his misery." Jaclyn told her dryly.

"We were talking about you," Jewel reminded her. "You need to give Tyler a break."

"Speaking of which," Savannah held up her ringing phone. "It's for you."

With a look that could kill, she grabbed the phone and went into the other room to take the call.

"Now back to you girl, what are you going to do about the situation you find yourself in?"

*****

"I am doing fine mom, honestly," Jewel tried not to sound impatient. The shop was packed with customers waiting to be served and even though she had hired two high school girls to work on Friday afternoons and Saturdays, she still liked to give them her personal touch. She was entering her fifth month and she was starting to show. A so she had started taking it a little easier. She had promised Jordan she would not overextend herself. "Mom, no you don't have to come here, I am fine and Jordan makes sure I am okay." She listened for a minute, smiling at the woman in front of her who needed her attention. "Mom, I have to talk to you later, I have customers. Okay, I love you too."

"Sorry about that, my mother is being overprotective." She told the middle aged woman as she handed her the book she had ordered.

"That's quite all right my dear. I am a mother myself." She said with a friendly smile. "And I see you are going to be one soon," her glance took in the slight bulge in her peach cashmere sweater.

"So I am," Jewel patted the slight bulge automatically.

"So you will know what it's like." With a wave she left the store with the package under her arm.

Jewel went back to dealing with some more of the customers and was busy helping a young lady to choose a book for her sister when he came in.

She did not know he was there until he was behind her. She had promised that she would go out to dinner with him later as soon as she closed the store. They were planning to go and eat at the little Italian restaurant near his office building.

She saw when the girl looked behind her and her gaze change to one of acute admiration. "I thought you said you would not be working so hard?" his deep voice said behind her.

"Jordan!" she turned to face him and her heart turned over by how handsome he was. He was all in black and his hair had been tousled by the wind. She could smell his elusive and expensive cologne. "What are you doing here?"

"Checking up on you, and see that you are breaking the promise you made to me." He must have noticed that all the women in the store were haggling him, including the two teenagers, but he was looking at her only. She felt a warmth of feeling special, run through her.

"I am taking it easy." She told him.

"I'll wait for you right by the corner." He pointed to the little corner table with the stool next to the window. "Sorry to interrupt," he told the girl behind them with a pleasant smile.

"No trouble at all," she told him, giving him a come hither look which passed right over him.

"You are a very lucky woman," she said with a sigh as soon as Jordan was out of earshot.

Jewel looked over at him as he sat on the stool, her expression thoughtful.

# Chapter 6

He wanted her to move in with him. She was now into her sixth month and they had found out that she was going to be having a girl.

They were at her apartment because they had just gotten in from a drive in the countryside. It was spring, and the flowers were in full bloom. He had called and told her to put on something warm, as they were going out to commune with nature.

"I am not ready yet." She told him stubbornly. She preferred this arrangement. She got to see him as much as possible but she still had her own space.

"You spend almost the entire nights at my place and some of your things are over here so why can't you move over?" he was pacing the length of the small living room, his hands shoved into the pockets of his denim.

"Because I want to have my own space where I can be by myself Jordan, I wish you could understand that." Jewel made her way into the kitchen to make a pot of tea. She hated arguing with him and wished he would just accept her position.

ve you, and you are carrying my child Jewel," he had followed her into the kitchen and stood behind her. "I want us to be a family Jews, and I get frustrated that you cannot see that."

She turned around to face him, discovering that he was very close to her.

"How long are you going to keep punishing me?" he asked her lifting her chin to look at her closely. "How long am I going to have to pay for what happened in the past?"

She felt her heart lurch inside her. She had been trying to put it behind her, but she could still recall the loneliness, the fear, and the extreme pain of losing their child that time several years ago, and somehow she could not move past it. He had also told her about the mistress his father had stashed somewhere, and she kept thinking about that poor woman who loved and lost.

"I need time," she whispered, her eyes pleading with him. "I need more time Jordan, please. I have some issues that I am dealing with and I just need to sort them out."

Page 96

"We are in this thing together, and I am so sad that you cannot see that." He told her wearily, his thumb caressed her cheek. "I am tired Jewel. I want my family with me and I was cheated of that all those years ago. I am sick of this arrangement. I have been tiptoeing around the subject of you living with me. I want to marry you and have my family with me. Is that so wrong?"

Her heart skittered at the word 'marry' and she wanted to shout yes but something was stopping her. She could not commit, not just yet.

"It's not wrong," she went into his arms and rested her head on his chest as he closed his arms around her. "I just want to make sure that this is something we both need Jordan. I am scared of feeling the way I did before and I don't want to lose control like that ever again."

"You are saying that loving me means losing control?" he eased her away from him to look down at her. "It's the opposite for me. Loving you makes me strong and it's the best thing that has ever happened to me." He tilted her head up and kissed her hungrily, eliciting a response from her as the desire stirred inside her and curled in her stomach. "I am going to give you some time to think about what I am asking you. I have to go away for a week on a business trip and when I come back, if you have changed your mind please let me know." He paused. "If you still feel the same way then I promise that I will always be there for you and our daughter."

"Jordan what are you saying?" she felt a frisson of fear going through her.

"I love you baby, but I need more. I need everything Jews, or nothing at all. I will leave a number where you can reach me in case of anything." He moved away from her and made his way towards the front door. "I love you Jewel, more than I can ever explain to you. I never stopped, even when I was away. I tried to forget you and put everything behind me but it did not work. I will love you until I die."

After he left, the silence in the apartment was deafening. She should not have let him go! She thought in panic. She jumped as she heard the whistling of the kettle signaling that the water was ready to prepare her tea.

She wanted to go after him but she felt glued to the floor with the memories racing through her mind.

"How about I carry those books for you?" he had come out of nowhere. Jaclyn and Savannah had gone ahead of her because they said they wanted to go look at some jeans at the mall before going home.

"Jordan! You scared me." She had stopped and looked at him as he walked up beside her. He was in his football jersey and his hair was falling on his forehead and he looked like he always did: handsome, carefree and totally irresistible.

"Did not mean to do that," he told her with a grin, reaching for the books in her hands. She gave them to him and he walked alongside her. "You have been avoiding me." He commented quietly.

"I have been busy with final exams." She avoided his gaze, not wanting to tell him he was right. Ever since he had kissed her a week ago she had found that she could not stop thinking about him. She had been doing a lot of talking to herself. He was a McIntyre and that means he was way out of her league and she noticed how all the girls hung around him. She had also heard talk that his parents did not tolerate African Americans. It was fine when they were employees, but one dating their only son was not going to be accepted.

"So have I, but I still have time to think about you." He held her arm, forcing her to stop. They were in the woods near her house and he led her off to the dense area where they could not be seen by anyone on the streets. "What are you afraid of?"

"Let's see," she pretended to think. "You are white and rich and I am black and live on the area of town where the people all work for your family. Besides that, you have probably been with every popular girl in school. Reasons enough?"

"No," he had told her softly. He had pulled her into his arms and her books had fallen to the ground as he bent his head to take her lips with his. "I cannot stop thinking about you and the way you taste when I kiss you. I have not been with anyone else since that time and I don't want to." He touched his mouth to her innocent one and she opened up for him. She had been like a flower opening up to accept the much needed nectar and as his tongue entered her mouth she had put her arms around his neck and clung to him weakly. He had pulled her closer and every sane reason she had drilled inside her mind as to why this was insane, slowly drifted away as he deepened the kiss.

It was at that moment that she realized that she did not want to stay away from him. No matter how far apart they were socially and financially, surely they could find a way to make it work.

He released her mouth slowly but he still held her close to him, the books scattered around the room forgotten, as they stared at each other, brown eyes staring into intense green as they transmitted their feelings for each other in the stillness of the woods. The only sounds were the beating of their hearts and some birds chirping in the trees around them.

"We belong together and nothing is going to keep us apart." he had told her hoarsely, his forehead resting against hers, his breath fanning her face. "Never forget that!" he added.

*****

"How about this one?" Jaclyn held up a cute pink onesie that said 'I am adorable' on it. It was Wednesday evening and they were at the mall shopping for baby clothes. She had not heard from Jordan and she found herself twisting and turning in bed because she was missing him so much. She had the number to call him but had decided against it. He needed to hear something that she was not prepared to say yet. She still did not know what to say to him. She nodded. He had told her that he wanted to foot every bill but she had told him no and he had gone ahead without her knowledge and deposit a sum of money into her account. When she had checked her balance she had placed her hand over her heart in shock to see the amount of money he had deposited there.

"Girl you look a mess. Why don't you call him?" Savannah asked her impatiently coming up behind them with her arms filled with a variety of baby clothes.

"I can't; at least not yet. I don't know what to tell him."

"I know what you should tell him," Savannah dumped the clothes into the basket. "You should call him up and tell him that you love him and it is miserable without him and that you are sorry for being such a dumb ass for not seeing it long before now."

"Thanks," Jewel said dryly.

"That's what friends are for." She said with a grin.

"She is right you know," Jaclyn was studying a pack of receivers and looking at the colors. "Look at me and Tyler, we are inseparable now, and at one time I thought I wanted nothing to do with him. I have met his parents and now we are practically engaged. You and Jordan are epic and as much as I hated him when I thought he had played you back then; I have to admit that, girl, for a white guy he sure is okay. I have never seen love like the two of you have. What the hell are you doing messing with that?"

"I am scared," Jewel admitted. "I keep remembering that time especially when I was in the hospital and called for him over and over again and he was not there. It's like I expect it to happen again."

"You know that that is irrational fear and you need to find a way to deal with it, and fast." Jaclyn told her seriously. "That man loves you and you love him, stop trying to complicate things more than it is."

*****

That evening while she was at the apartment putting away the clothes and other things she had bought, along with the ones her friends had bought for their goddaughter, she heard a knock on the door. For an insane moment she thought it was Jordan and maybe he had come back early after all. A look through the peephole and to her surprise she discovered that it was Jordan's mother, Caroline.

She pulled the door open and stood there looking at her, not even aware that the woman knew where she lived. She had a large gift bag in her hand, which she handed to Jewel. "Something for my granddaughter." She said with a smile.

"Come on in," Jewel held the door opened wider to let her in. She had not seen or spoken to her since Jordan had left.

"You must be wondering what I am doing here," she was nervous and Jewel could tell by the way she twisted the straps of her designer bag in her hands.

"You were in the neighborhood?" Jewel asked with a straight face, indicating that she have a seat on one of the small sofas.

"Good one," the woman said with a short laugh as she took her seat. Jewel sat opposite her and waited for her to talk. "I have not heard from Jordan, have you?"

"No, but he left a number in case I need to get in touch with him." Jewel suddenly felt sorry for her. She looked so lost and alone.

"He still has not forgiven me and his father for what we did to you both." Caroline stretched out her immaculately clad legs in front of her.

"I am sure he will," Jewel assured her.

"I was born in a very poor part of town and thought I would never get out." She looked down at the pocketbook she had in her hands. "I was an only child and I should have felt special, but my father was a mean drunk and my mother was a very weak woman who took everything that was handed to her without murmur and she just looked on while he started using his fists on me. I ran away when I was sixteen and never looked back. I spent three years on the streets living in old cars, until I decided that I needed something more. I was working in a strip club serving drinks when Jordan's father started noticing me; he started taking me out and grooming me to be his wife. At first I was excited because I finally had what I wanted, a rich man who could keep me in the lifestyle I had craved, but he never loved me; I was one of his possessions, or more like one of the broken down companies he bought and fixed up, only he did not sell me to the highest bidder, because he was the highest bidder." She blinked back the tears. "I pretended to be happy and use shopping as my therapy and whenever I go out to functions with him, I would smile and look my best so that people would not see the pathetic unhappy woman from small town USA."

Jewel finally understood what had driven her to act the way she did in the past. She had let her insecurities and the desperate need to gain her husband's approval, color her views, and she felt sorry for her. What a horrible life!

"I found out recently that my husband, who had been so big on respect and sticking to his own kind, had been seeing a colored woman," she looked up at Jewel in apology and the girl shook her head letting her know she was not offended. "Her name is Sally and he bought her a string of beauty salons some years ago." She smiled sadly.

"I found some receipts in a desk drawer that had been locked for years. There were also letters that she wrote him, letting him know that no matter what she will always love him and that even though he had had her kill their child, she was still going to love him. She had been pregnant with his child, and all this time I thought that even though he did not love me, at least he respected me. Now I realize that I never had his love and certainly not his respect." She leaned forward and took

Jewel's hands in hers, surprising the girl. "Jordan is not like his father, he is kind, loving and a perfect gentleman. He certainly did not get it from either of us," she said with a grim smile. "He loves you. I have wished with all the money and fine clothes and jewelry that I have in my possession, that I had that. He loves you and for him there can be no one else; don't lose that."

"I won't," Jewel gripped her hands with her own. "There has never been anyone else for me but him either and never will be."

"Thanks for listening and for forgiving me for what I did." She smiled sadly. "I just hope my son will be able to forgive me one day."

"He will," Jewel said with a certainty borne from knowing the man she loved.

*****

It was ten o'clock that night before she called the number. He answered on the second ring and it was obvious that he had been sleeping. "Jewel, what's wrong?" his tone sounded urgent.

"I am okay and so is your daughter," she assured him. "I just wanted to hear your voice, I miss you."

"I miss you too," he told her huskily.

"Your mother came to see me today."

"What did she say? Did she upset you?" she heard it, the protectiveness, and that told her everything she needed to know. She realized that this man was a man who was never going to let anything or anyone hurt her, no matter who they were.

"She did not upset me." She told him softly. "We just talked Jordan, that's all. When are you coming home?"

"On Friday. Is something wrong, Jews? You sound weird." There was concern in his deep voice.

"Yes something is wrong. I am aching for you and I need you beside me; inside me, and I don't want you to leave me like that again."

There was silence at the other end and Jewel smiled as she envisioned his reaction. "I have a meeting in the morning." His voice was hoarse. "I am coming home after that. Jews I need you right now."

"I need you too." She told him huskily. "I am in bed right now and I opening my nightgown. My hand is going between my legs and I am pretending that it is you parting them. My legs are wide open now, I close my eyes and I can feel your tongue inside me, thrusting inside me."

She heard his deep groan over the phone lines and she felt the lick of desire coursing through her. "I love you Jordan McIntyre and I have loved you all my life; I want only you. I love what you do when you are on top of me and your mouth is on my nipples."

"I am inside you now baby, feel me, feel the way I am pushing myself inside you, deeper and deeper until I can touch your soul. My thrusts have become more urgent and I feel you moving with me, we are on the brink of coming together." He breathed harshly. "Can you feel it?"

Jewel touched her nipple, hard from his words and ran a finger over it. "Yes," she gasped.
"Stay with me baby, and let me guide you through this." He told her urgently.

"Jordan,' she whimpered as she felt herself weakened.

"Are you ready?" he asked her.

"Yes," she whispered as the feeling washed over her. It was so intense, like he was right on top of her and she cried out his name as he whispered to her, assuring her that he was right there.

She fell asleep with his voice in her ear and her hand on her bulging stomach.

*****

She was in the store with customers when he came in the next day. He stood there in the doorway looking at her, his green eyes devouring her as she stood there talking to the customer. "Could you excuse me for a moment?" she asked, barely able to be civil. Without waiting for the woman's reply, she made her way over to him, not caring who was looking. He did not come to her but waited for her to come to him, and she did, wrapping hr arms around his neck and drinking in his beloved face. The wind had tousled his hair and the dark blue shirt he was wearing highlighted his deep tan. "Welcome, back darling," she said huskily.

"I missed you." He murmured, his arms going around her. "I need you right now," he told her huskily. "Do you have someone to take over for you?"

"If I don't, I will just close the place," she told him, her arms still tight around his neck. " I will just call Savannah to come and take over for me."

"Do that and let's get out of here."

# Chapter 7

He took her to his place. It was only half past four when they got there. He had driven all the way, with his hand holding hers on his thigh as if afraid she was going to vanish into thin air if he let her go. Savannah had just left work and she came straight over, giving an approving nod as she saw Jordan standing there waiting. "Don't screw it up," she had whispered when Jewel got ready to leave.

He drove around to the side entrance and she noticed that the gardener was busily pruning the hedges located around the back. The scent of flowers wafted in the air giving the atmosphere an aroma that was pleasing to the senses.

"Are you hungry?" he took off his light spring jacket and hung it up, taking hers to do the same.

"We can eat later," she told him softly coming over to put her arms around his neck.

"You're right." He murmured. "All the way here I kept thinking about last night. I have been hard ever since." He lifted her up and took her into the bedroom, placing her gently on the bed. "I never stopped loving you Jews, even when I was not around." He had taken off his shirt and was pulling the buckle of his leather belt. "You are an extension of me and that is the part I cannot do without." He flung the belt on the carpeted floor and it made a faded thud. "I berated myself for giving you that ultimatum, because the truth is I cannot be without you." He stood before her, gloriously naked, his erection pulsating, the tip red and shiny from the little beads of moisture gathered there. Her gaze was riveted and she found that she could not look away. She wanted it inside her mouth, to taste and to savor.

She lifted her gaze to his and he knew exactly what she wanted without her having to say it. He had taught her the art of pleasuring him there. The first time she had almost gagged as she swallowed the length of him, but he had gently held himself and fed her a little bit at a time. He undressed her and when she was totally naked, he positioned himself over her face, guiding his erection to her lips. Her tongue reached out and she licked the tip, reaching for the small opening there. He groaned softly. She then opened her mouth and took him in. She removed his hand and replaced it with hers and took him a little bit at a time inside her mouth, her teeth grazing him just a little bit. She had risen to her elbows and her eyes held his as she took him further inside her mouth. He thrust into her gently, his teeth clenched as the combination of her teeth and tongue threatening to drive him crazy! She reached underneath to put a little pressure on his testicles and he called out her name harshly, his body shuddering with the exquisite pleasure racing through him. He was not going to make it, he thought, as he felt his body losing control. With a tortured groan he pulled out of her mouth and quickly entered her vagina, his penis made slippery by her saliva. He started thrusting inside her rapidly, his breathing irregular. He felt as if he was going to have a heart attack, the way his heart was pounding inside his chest. With a mumbled oath he reached for one of her nipples and pulled it inside his mouth, sucking and tasting as if he would die without it. Jewel bent her knees and opened wider for him, her nails digging into his firm buttocks as she returned his thrusts with her own desperate ones.

He knew she was about to explode because he felt it within himself as well and with a feral groan he released her nipple and took her lips with his. He met her halfway, their cries captured inside each other's mouths, their bodies shuddering with the power of an orgasm that rocked them to the very core!

He still held her lips with his as their bodies tried to recover from the passion that had almost overwhelmed them. She still clung to him, her legs holding him captive as she returned the kiss.

He released her lips finally and rested his forehead against hers, trying to control his breathing. "You okay?" he asked her gently.

"Ask me again in another few minutes," she told him softly. She brushed back the hair from his forehead, her eyes meeting his.

"Am I hurting you?" he asked her anxiously, getting ready to move off her.

"No," she held him to her. "I just want to hold you for a little bit more. I missed you so much when you were gone that I had flashbacks to when you had left before." She felt him stiffen on top of her and realized that she had stirred up some bad memories. "It's okay Jordan," she rested her hands on his jaw and lifted his head to look at her. "We are past that now and I promise you that I no longer blame you for what happened. I love you and always will, no matter what."

"I just want to erase the past," he moved off her and she felt bereft, but he gathered her close to him, putting her head on his chest. "I have to tell you something," he clasped her hand that was resting on his chest and took a deep breath. "I have been with quite a few women in my quest to forget you. I keep thinking about that and feel ashamed; it was like I had cheated on you, and I cannot forgive myself for that; I don't know how." His voice was raspy with regret and lifting her head Jewel saw the raw emotions on his face.

"There is nothing to forgive," she told him softly. "If it happens now then there will be hell to pay!"

*****

They talked and reminisced about the past when they had been in a much better place.

"Remember when we were studying for that literature exam?" he mused. She was spread half over his chest, the sprinkling of hair tickling her cheek.

"You mean when we were reading 'Pride and Prejudice'?" she asked him mildly, a soft smile on her face as the memory became distinct. "You reached underneath my shirt and started fondling me and I lost all sense of what I was reading."

"Doing that was much more interesting than reading about some old stuck up guy who had a lot of difficulty telling the woman that he was into her." He told her with a grin.

"Mr. Bingley was a gentleman who wanted to wait for the opportune time to let Jane know how interested he was." Jewel lifted her head to look at him. "It's a wonder you did not fail the exam."

"I am a literary genius," he touched the fine hairs at her temple. "And I had a great teacher." She bent her head and kissed him tenderly. They had not bothered to put on any clothes. He reached between them and started fingering her mound. She opened up for him and he dipped two fingers inside her, thrusting inside as she squeezed and moved against his fingers, her lips becoming hungry and desperate. He did not stop until she had come all over him, her whimpers echoing around the room.

*****

She moved in with him even though he had not asked her again. Her friends helped her pack the stuff she needed and she was going to lease the apartment out to a college student who had asked her.

"I have so many good memories of this place," Jaclyn said staring around the bedroom with its brightly colored walls. "That ding in the wall was when we were moving the armoire and putting it over there."

"You are right and you told me it was Savannah who did it," Jewel looked at her friend and shook her head. She had called her mother and told her what was happening, and she had asked her about marriage? "I am not ready yet, mom."

"Honey, moving on with a man is as much a commitment as moving in with him." she had said.

"And remember the time when we got drunk and Jaclyn threw up in that corner, nearest to the bed?" Savannah asked sending her friend a triumphant look.

"I was not drunk!" Jaclyn protested folding the towel neatly and putting it into the container. "It was something I ate."

"Yeah right," Savannah said sardonically. "Girls, do you realize that this is the end of an era?"

"What do you mean?" Jewel asked her abandoning her folding of nightgowns and sitting on the bed.

"It means that we are no longer going to be able to hang out like we use to do." Savannah told her. "You are about to pop and now you are going to be living with Jordan; and Jaclyn spends so much time over at Tyler's place that she is practically living there; and well, Blake and I are inching around trying to decide on the next step in our relationship. Things are changing between us."

"No matter who is in our lives, we are still going to remain friends. We have been through too much together." Jewel said firmly.

"Let's toast to that." Jaclyn went into the kitchen to get a box of orange juice and some wine glasses. "Friends forever."

"Friends forever," the other two girls agreed.

*****

It felt strange living with him. His mother had come up to welcome her, and her and Jordan had settled into a tentative relationship. She was bending over backwards to right the wrong that she had helped to do in the past.

The first night he had brought home pizza they had sat on the carpet in the living room and ate many slices and drank orange juice. She had been afraid to spill anything on the obviously expensive carpet until he had deliberately let a piece of bacon and cheese fall onto it. "Jordan, what have you done?" she had cried agitatedly.

"It's just stuff baby," he had told her solemnly, reaching over to kiss her on the lips. "We have stain remover for this and if not it can be replaced."

She started getting up and he realized that she was getting ready to go and look for the stain remover.

"Don't you dare!" he had said with a laugh, holding on to her hand. "It can be a reminder of our first night together."

They had made love slow and leisurely same place in the living room where he had spread a blanket on the carpet to stop her from getting carpet burn.

They were very different. She had always been neat and tidy, folding away her stuff as soon as she took them off but Jordan dropped his clothes on the floor in the bathroom and left them there. The first time she had seen him do it she had taken it up and put it in the hamper. The next time it happened she had confronted him about it and told him she was not his helper. "What are you talking about?" he had asked her puzzled. "I don't expect you to pick up after me baby; we have people who do that."

She had stared at him in disbelief and it had been brought home to her how different they had been brought up. People had been picking up after him his entire life and he was accustomed to it. "So that gives you the right to drop your clothes on the floor, because you have someone stupid or desperate enough for the money, you pay them to pick them up?" she had rounded on him furiously, her hands on her hips.

"I can't believe you said that," he had stared at her, noticing her parted lips and her baby bump and her glowingly exquisite face. He loved living with her and he raced home everyday to be with her. "We always treat our employees very fair Jewel, you only need to ask them."

"Pick up your stuff Jordan; I am not going to pretend not to see them, and if I have to pick them up I am going to throw them in the trash can." She told him.

"Okay baby, you are the boss." He had told her quietly.

*****

"He is messy," Jewel said sitting down carefully on the chair in Savannah's living room. Jordan had gone to a business dinner and had wanted her to accompany him but she had declined, telling him she was feeling a little tired; and besides, she wanted to spend some time with her friends. It was almost the end of May and she was getting bigger by the day. "Thanks," she accepted the glass of lemonade from her friend gratefully.

"Ah, the joys of living with a man," Savannah said with a grin taking a seat on one of the sofas scattered around the large airy bedroom. "Been there honey. That's what's keeping me from saying yes to Blake."

"I sound like a nagging wife and we are not even married." Jewel grumbled.

"Just tell him the truth." Jaclyn suggested. She was sitting there cradling a glass of lemonade in her hands and had curled her feet underneath her. It was Saturday night and they had met for their usual chat.

"I did," Jewel said with a shrug. "I told him about throwing his clothes on the floor for the helpers to pick them up, but it's not only that. He makes a mess in the kitchen when he cooks dinner for us and does not clean it up. I feel badly for the helpers there so when he has gone to bed I end up going into the kitchen and clean up. It's exhausting."

"Do you love him?" Jaclyn asked her quietly.

Jewel looked at her friend in surprise. "Of course I do, there is no doubt about that."

"Then you are going to have to compromise. This sort of thing is new to him and he is learning about you as well. But talk to him and tell him how you feel and hear what he has to say." Jaclyn told her wisely.

*****

"What don't you like about me?" she asked him that night while they were in bed. He had called her and told her he was leaving the dinner and if she wanted him to pick her up. She had told him yes and he had come over.

"What a question!" she was spread over his chest with his arms around her. "I love everything about you."

"I am serious Jordan," she raised her head to look down at him and his amazing green eyes met hers. "I want honesty between us and that means everything, not just the big things, but the little things as well."

"Okay," he said slowly, seeing that she was very serious. "I hate that you refuse to accept anything of worth from me, like that diamond necklace I wanted to get you and the several other things I want to buy you; and I hate that you think my wealth is something not to be proud of. I also hate that you won't accept that we have people working for us. I know you grew up in a home that was not as opulent as this one Jewel, but you have accepted me and you have to accept that I am a very wealthy man. It is not a sin to be rich."

She stared down at him and realized that she had been doing just that. Trying to disassociate herself from what he represents, even to the point of not going to his fancy dinners and refusing to wear the expensive clothes he had bought her.

"It's your turn," he told her quietly.

"It's going to make me sound petty if I tell you, she murmured.

"Tell me just the same, honesty and all that," he told her lightly.

"You are messy. I get it that you are used to having people pick up after you all your life but I am not used to that and it gets on my nerves. The helpers that work here have this big mansion to take care of without them having to walk behind you and do all that." She looked at him to see his reaction.

"Maude," he said referring to a plump middle aged African American woman who was the head housekeeper. "She was more of a mother to me than my own mother and she disciplined me when I needed it. I was six years old when I started calling her mom. My mother wanted my dad to fire her but my dad told her that if she had been playing her part, I would not have to call another woman mom. Irene," he was referring to the tall slender Scottish woman who mostly did work for his mother. "does not take crap from any of us and is not afraid to speak her mind. The other two and Stefan the cook are basically the same, they treat me like their child instead of the master of the house and they cater to my needs because they love me. But you are right. I grew up privileged and I am used to being catered to. From now on I will try and do better."

"Do I sound like a nag?" she asked him anxiously.

"A little bit," he said with a teasing grin. "Ouch," he murmured as she punched him lightly in his flat stomach. "I love you Jewel and whatever it takes to make you happy, I am up for it."

*****

Caroline knew she was trying too hard but she had gotten a second chance and she was grabbing it with both hands. Her son was relating to her better these days, thanks to Jewel, the same girl she had caused so much misery to in the past. She had gone out and practically bought out the whole baby store but she was worried that Jewel was going to be upset that she had taken it upon herself to do it.

She had invited her friends over to help decorate the nursery, refusing to get a professional when Caroline had suggested it.

She was already seven months pregnant and had started cutting back her hours at the bookstore because she had hired someone to help her out there. It was Saturday afternoon. Jordan had taken her out for breakfast and brought her back and then had gone to play golf with some friends. "You are so white," she had teased him as he lugged his golf clubs down to his vehicle.

"I am not!" he had retorted. "I am in love with a sister, aren't I?"

"You are so not pulling that off," Jewel had told him dryly.

"I just need some more practice." He told her, giving her a kiss on the lips before leaving.

The girls were on their way over. She had gone into the room designated to be the nursery when Caroline came in. "Hi," Jewel looked up in surprise. "I thought you had a luncheon with your friends."

"They are not my friends," Caroline corrected her. "And I would rather be decorating my granddaughter's nursery than being out with a bunch of phonies." She paused a little bit. "I am afraid I have gone and done something you might not approve of."

"Like what?" Jewel looked at her curiously. They now shared a tentative relationship but it was getting better every day.

She stepped back and allowed several people to come inside the room. There were about ten women and they were all bearing several large bags from a baby store she knew sold only the most expensive things. "I went overboard and practically bought out the entire store."

Jewel stared at the mounting number of packages and her eyes widened as she realized that they had gone for more.

"Do you mind?" she asked anxiously.

"This baby is going to have more clothes than all of us combined," Jewel said in amusement, not in the least bit offended. As a matter of fact she was touched at how much Caroline was doing to make up for the past.

"I am far from being offended." She told the older woman softly, going over to give her a brief hug which had her staring at Jewel in amazement.

"Thank you," she murmured softly returning the hug.

By the time her friends got there, both of them were knee deep in soft tissue papers.

# Chapter 8

Jordan stared at the ring in his hand. It was a square cut diamond that shone in the dim light in his office. He had bought it several months ago and was waiting for the right opportunity to give it to her.

She had not mentioned marriage to him since they had been living together for the past two months. She was eight months pregnant now and swollen with his child and all he wanted to do was to have his ring on her finger and his name added to hers. He wanted his family. Living with her and making love to her every night did not make her his wife, he wanted more.

"Oh my gosh! That's a beautiful ring!" He had been so engrossed in his thoughts that he had not heard her come in.

"I knocked and when I did not hear you, I came in." the secretary apologized. "So I take it congratulations are in order?"

Jordan snapped the box shut, irritated that he had allowed anyone to see it before her. He looked at the secretary as if he was seeing her for the first time. She must be around his mother's age, blonde blue eyes and very attractive and well preserved. His sharp eyes noticed her subtle expensive peach suit and her well groomed hair. They were very well paid at the company but he also noticed discreet diamond earrings in her lobe.

"Have a seat Marjorie," he indicated for her to sit on one of the chairs available in front of the desk. "Was it worth it?"

I beg your pardon?" her light blue eyes stared into his green ones.

"How long did the affair last?" he asked her.

She shifted her gaze and settled it on her clasped hands. "I have no idea what you are talking about."

"I have flashbacks of when I was a teenager and used to come to the office with my dad." He leaned back in the soft leather chair and gave her his full attention. "I blocked it out for years because I did not want to believe that my father was a cliché. I take it you were well compensated for the time? Clothes, jewelry, expense account and a car, but was it worth it?"

"I loved him!" she cried, her blue eyes welling up with tears. "I did everything for him and he promised me-"her voice tapered off and she could not look at him.

"He promised you he would leave his wife and kid and marry you." Jordan finished the sentence grimly. He rest his head back against the soft leather, suddenly very weary and realized that he would have to replace all the furnishings in the office. "You knew he was seeing someone else? An African American woman the same time he was seeing you?"

She looked up at him startled. "He told me I was the only one," she said tremulously the tears falling down her cheeks.

"And you believe a man who was cheating on his wife with you, that you were the only one," Jordan sighed wearily. "How long?"

"He hired me when I was twenty-two years old and he seduced me two months after." Her lips trembled pitifully. "I fell in love with him soon after."

Jordan looked at her and tried not let the contempt he felt for her to show. His father had been his hero when he was a young boy growing up and he had thought he wanted to be like him. He had given him a woman to have sex with on his sixteenth birthday and had told him to explore away, she was paid for until the morning and he had thought he had the coolest father ever. Now he knew different and all he felt for him now was contempt and derision. The man had been a pathetic womanizer who used women to satisfy his baser needs and paid them off with material things.

"Are you going to fire me?" Marjorie asked him tentatively.

Jordan looked at her. He had almost forgotten she was there.

"You are very efficient and know the running of the company; I am not so stupid as to think that I don't need that." He told her brusquely. "You stay for now." With a wave of his hand he dismissed her, just wanting to be alone for a little bit.

"Thank you Mr. McIntyre." She hurriedly left the office and closed the door behind her.

He stared sightlessly at the mural in front of him. He wondered if he was eventually going to be like his father. Was it why he hesitated to bring up marriage again to Jewel? He knew he loved her more than life itself but what if after the marriage had been seasoned he decided that he needed more? Was he going to hurt her eventually? He had slept with other women while he had been in Europe but he had always used protection, unconsciously knowing that he only wanted to have a family with one woman and her name was Jewel.

What if he ended up hurting her?

*****

Jewel gave the package to the girl with a smile and a wave. She was going home shortly just as soon as Jordan came to pick her up. He had called and told her he would be by to pick her up in the next ten minutes. It was already June and the summer had been mild so far with a few scattering of showers. The nursery had been decorated and she had spent several nights just looking at the beautiful peach and cream décor and she had played the music on the mobile several times.

The phone rang just as she was about to reach for her pocket book. "Hi mom how are you?

"I am fine honey I just got in from the pool. It is so hot you will never believe it. So how is my granddaughter doing?"

"She is doing great mom." Jewel settled on the stool, cradling the phone against her ear as she searched for her set of keys for the store. "When are you coming over?"

"Honey, I am coming before you drop your load don't worry about it."

"I can't wait to see you." Jewel told her.

"I know you don't to hear what your old mom has to say but what about marriage? You know I did not raise you to be shacking up with any man."

"Mom we are not ready yet. We are trying to get the feel of living in the same space right now."

"What does Jordan say?"

"He has not said anything to me since I moved in so maybe he is okay with the arrangement."

"What are you afraid of baby girl?" her mother asked her quietly.

"I am not afraid of anything but I just want to get accustomed to living with him and make sure that this is what he really wants."

"So you are doing this for him?"

"As well as for me." Jewel's voice was defensive and she was tired of trying to explain herself to her mother and her friends. She needed time.

"You love each other Jewel and the ultimate commitment is getting married. If you are not sure about him, you should let him know now and not wait until he starts resenting you for not loving him enough to give him your total commitment."

*****

"You are quiet. What's going on?" he asked her as soon as they were half way home.
"I am just tired that's all." She told him with a forced smile. After she had finished talking to her mother, there had not been enough time for her to process the conversation because he had come for her just then.

He reached across and placed his hand over her bulging stomach. "I want to feel our daughter kick," he told her softly, driving one handed and looking at her briefly. "I am going to be responsible for a life and I don't want to screw it up."

"You are not going to screw it up." She placed her hand over his and they both felt it at the same time, the movement of the child inside her womb.

"I am going to be a father," he said shakily pulling the car to a stop inside the circular driveway. "I want to get it right."

\*\*\*\*\*

"Can you tell me what's bothering you?" she asked him as soon as he climbed into the bed beside her. He had helped her showered and they had had dinner with his mother.

He closed his hand around her as she settled on his chest. "I am afraid I am going to turn out like my father." He told her solemnly. He told her of the conversation he had had with the secretary and how he remembered things from the past that made him realize that he had been having an affair with her as well. "I find myself thinking about him a lot and how I used to think he was my hero and how much I wanted to be like him.

He was a womanizer Jewel, and I am wondering if I am going to be like him."

"And I beg to differ," she lifted her head to look at him and his green eyes met hers. "You are a wonderful and loving man and you have been in love with the same woman since you were a teenager."

"So is there another reason why you won't marry me?" he asked her quizzically.

"There is," she told him with a gentle smile, her hand tracing the dimple in his chin. "I want a fairy tale wedding with a billowing chiffon gown and the whole works and I cannot have that when I have this." She patted her stomach. "And I want our daughter to be in the wedding photo with us. I want to marry you Jordan and I know for a fact that you are going to be the best husband a girl could ever wish for and I am willing to wait for that day when I can walk up the aisle to meet you, not waddle with someone having to hold me in case I fall."

"Why didn't you tell me all this before?" he switched position and propped her up against the pillows on the bed with him looking down at her.

"Because at first I was afraid. I was afraid that you would find that maybe you had made a mistake and you would be just doing it because I was carrying your child. You only said it to me once and when I moved in here with you, there was no mention of it again." She rested her hand against his jaw and felt the rough growth of hair there.

"You know that will never be the case." He bent his head to kiss her softly on the mouth. "I love you Jewel and it will always be you and no one else."

"So that answers your question. You are nothing like your father." She brought down his head and took his lips with hers. "I love you Jordan McIntyre."

\*\*\*\*\*

"Why did you put up with his Infidelities mother?" Jordan asked his mother. They were in the living room having lemonade and talking. Jewel had gone to lunch with her friends and he had not gone in to the office; he had stopped going in on Saturdays.

Caroline placed her lemonade glass on the coaster on the glass table. She had been waiting for him to ask her that question ever since his father had died. "I thought I loved him." she said quietly. "I was dazzled by him, his wealth and his charm and I wanted better for my life and he offered it to me."

"I will never get how a woman put up with a man who has little or no regard for her." He had been trying to figure it out for himself and he had been determined to mend fences with her. He had forgiven her but there were still some issues to be sorted out.

"I knew he was cheating and I ignored it, by telling myself that as long as I had all this," she gestured around the opulent room. "then I would be okay. I convince myself of it so much that I found myself believing it."

"I am not judging you mother; I am just trying to find myself in all this. I have asked Jewel to marry me and I want to make sure that I will never hurt her the way dad hurt you." He leaned forward and took her hands in his. "I want to be more than he was."

"You are," Caroline told him with a tremulous smile. "He was never the man you are because he had to prove to himself and to others that he was a powerful man and he went about doing it the wrong way."

"I appreciate you saying that mother," he squeezed her hands gently before letting go.

"So you asked Jewel to marry you?" She asked with a smile.

"I did." He smiled gently. "I love her so much mother that sometimes I find myself in a panic wondering if I am going to lose her."

"Your love has sustained a lot of obstacles and weathered so many storms and still remains strong. You two were made for each other, there is no doubt about that." Caroline told him with a wistful smile. "I envy that."

"Thank you mother." He told her gently, finally understanding what she had been through.

*****

"Jaclyn will you get off the phone!" Savannah called out to the girl. She was in the living room on the phone while she and Jewel were in the kitchen munching on pizza. "You just left Tyler a few minutes ago. What on earth do you have to talk to him about now?"

"We were making plans for tomorrow," Jaclyn said defensively putting away the phone. "I can't help it if I am irresistible."

"Irresistible, my ass! The man probably wants a piece of the tail you gave him earlier." Savannah said with a snort.

"Okay you two, play nice," Jewel said with a complacent smile. "Savannah, how is Blake?"

"He is there," she shrugged. "He wants to know if he can move into my apartment because that would mean saving him rent."

"I hope you told him no, honey." Jewel said to her.

"Of course I did!" Savannah bit into her pizza with gusto. "I told him there was no way I would ever fall for that again."

"I thought things were going so well." Jaclyn said to her.

"You were so wrapped up with Tyler that I did not have the heart to tell you that his friend had become a player." Savannah said.

"I am your friend Sav, and you know that means a lot to me." Jaclyn rebuked her. "So are you going to see him again?"

"I don't know." She said with a shrug. "He called and apologized and said he was out of line but I am not feeling it anymore. You two have found something special and I am happy for that and that's what I want, I don't want to settle anymore."

"Good for you honey." Jewel said giving her a hug.

*****

Caroline emptied the box on her bed. She had been holding on to the things James had had locked away in a desk drawer to remind herself of who he really was but now she realized that she no longer needed that. Watching her son and Jewel had taught her a lot. She had shortchanged herself and spent the greater part of her life with a man who had never loved her but had disrespected her every chance he got. There was his secret phone that he had put away every time she had come into the room and she had pretended not to notice. She had the numbers of the women he had been sleeping with and the giveaway text messages that they had shared. She knew about the secretary from the office and had thought about marching over there and telling her to get the hell out but she had thought better of it. They had been as much victims as she had been and what was worse was that the poor women had been in love with him.

She had given away all of his things after making sure that Jordan had no need for them but she wanted no reminder of him inside the suite. He had stopped having sex with her the last year of their marriage and when she had cried and asked him about it he had told her that it had nothing to do with her but everything to do with him. He had turned his back on her and gone to sleep leaving her staring up at the ceiling and wondering what she had done wrong.

She closed the box with a smile and realized that she was free of James McIntyre and she couldn't be happier!

*****

"How about Selena?" Jordan asked her. They were in the kitchen and she was making a salad to go with the steak he had prepared. She loved this, both of them working together as a couple and it gave her a warm feeling.

"I don't think so," she popped a piece of tomato inside his mouth as he leaned over to look at what she was doing. He had already set the table and was waiting for her to finish. His mother had gone out with friends and had told them she was going to have fun.

"Why not?" he asked her puzzled.

"I was thinking Jordanna Angela McIntyre." She looked up at him with a smile.

"So you have it all figured out, huh?" he asked her huskily.

"Hmm," she passed him the salad bowl. "We could call her Angel for short." She suggested.

"I love it." He took her hand and led her into the dining room.

She told him about Savannah and Blake. "I am glad you have been the only man for me Jordan. I think that is so special and I would never change that."

"You are the only woman for me, the others have been physical and I wished I could change it. I love you so much Jewel." He told her earnestly. "You said you want to wait until you have our daughter in order to get married but I want to give you this just the same." He opened the box he slid out of his pocket and opened it.

Jewel stared at it wordlessly, spellbound by the beauty of the single diamond. "I want to officially declare my love for you and I am asking you to wear my ring."

"I would be honored to." She told him huskily holding out her left hand for him to put the ring on her finger. "It's beautiful." She whispered.

"I wondered if you would think it was too much. I kept thinking I should go back and get a simpler one." He was kneeling in front of her.

"How long ago did you buy it?" she asked him curiously, looking down at the ring shining on her finger.

"Since I found out you were carrying my baby." He told her with a smile. He took her hand and turned it around, kissing her palm and left her tingling.

"And you had it all this time?" she looked at him in amazement.

"Hoping that one day you will say yes." He nodded.

"I am saying yes over and over again." She clasped her arms around his neck. "I will always say yes."

*****

That night she was the one who watched him sleep. They had eaten and he had done the dishes by himself, no longer leaving them inside the sink for the helpers to deal with. He had bathed her, rubbing the sponge gently all over her body and afterwards they had made slow passionate love in the bedroom.

She remembered once in their teenage years when he had brought her chocolates and flowers and how she had treasured them. He had told her he had wanted to buy her a diamond necklace but he knew she would not have accepted it.

"I want to give you so much Jewel, if you will let me." He had whispered to her as his hands wandered over her body. They had been in their favorite spot in the little wooded area, a little distance from his house. He had brought along a picnic basket along with the flowers and chocolate. "I love you and I want us to be together forever."

"You are starting to sound like a stalker," she had teased him.

With a soft sigh she rested her head on his chest and closed her eyes as his arms closed around her. She was where she belonged.

# Chapter 9

July came with sizzling heat and thunderstorms. Caroline had decided to throw an open barbecue and had sent out invitations to all her friends and acquaintances and most of the employees at McIntyre and Company. Jewel's mother had flown in from Florida and was staying with them for the time until the baby was born. It was promising to be quite a crush and Jewel was staying as far away as possible from the planning and the preparing of the 4$^{th}$ of July event, not that she was needed anyway. Caroline had hired the best caterers in town and besides those in the household she had also hired extra help to deal with the cleaning up and making sure everything was perfect. She and Sylvia had hit it off and were both supervising the preparation.

"How about breakfast in bed?" Jordan asked as soon as he came out of the bathroom. He was completely naked and was rubbing the dampness off his skin with a towel. She was still in bed because she felt tired and worn out. She had been having little twinges during the night but had read up on the whole birthing process, and knew it was not the real thing – yet.

"Sounds like a good idea." She was propped up on several pillows as she tried to get comfortable. "You weren't planning to go into the kitchen like that were you?" she teased him.

"Maybe," he came over and climbed the few steps that led up to the huge king sized bed and sat on the edge of it, his green eyes searching her face. He had felt her restlessness last night and had spent the night listening out if she had gone into labor. "You okay?" he brushed wisps of her hair off her forehead as he examined her closely.

"Yes, I am just a little bit uncomfortable." She told him with a smile. "Now, about that breakfast,"

"Coming right up," he kissed her gently on the mouth before going off to get dressed so he could prepare something for her.

*****

"Honey why don't you take a seat? You look like you are about to pop any second now." Sylvia guided her to a comfortable lawn chair and handed her a glass of ice cold lemonade. She had just come down after she had taken another nap after breakfast and had just woke up half an hour ago. Jordan had given her a shower and helped her get dressed.

It was close to midday and the tables and chair had been set up. There were gaily colored umbrellas over each table and several people milling around setting up the food area. "Thanks mom," Jewel said gratefully as she accepted the cold drink.

"Where is Jordan?" she asked, looking around the vast grounds.

"He was in his study making a few calls. I kind of interrupted a business meeting yesterday when he rushed home thinking I had gone into labor; now he refuses to even leave the house just in case I need to go to the hospital and he is not around."

"I am so proud of that young man," Sylvia said shaking her head and taking a seat beside her daughter. "He has taken his responsibilities seriously and I notice how his eyes follow you wherever you are." She sighed and leaned back against the chair. Her mother had taken to wearing flamboyant and colorful wigs and when Jewel had asked her about it she had told her that all her friends in Florida were wearing them. Jewel looked like her a great deal and they were often mistaken for sisters. "I had something like that with your father," she continued with a whimsical smile. "Robert is all right, and he treats me like a man is supposed to treat a woman, but your father was the love of my life and no one can ever replace that."

"Is that fair to Robert?" Jewel asked her curiously. She did not think she could ever be with any one apart from Jordan and even the thought of it made her want to panic.

"We understand each other honey and we are very good companions, and more than that we are very good friends. That's what's important at our age."

"I love Jordan so much; I have loved him all my life, it has become like breathing to me." Jewel said with a small smile. "He will always be the only man for me."

"That's beautiful honey and very few people have that." Sylvia reached over and squeezed her hand gently.

*****

"I had no idea this place was so huge!" Savannah exclaimed, flopping down on a chair next to Jewel. They were all sitting beside the pool and both Savannah and Jaclyn had brought Tyler and Blake. Savannah had decided to give Blake another chance. "If he screws up again he's gone for good." She had said grimly.

Jordan had gone to get Jewel something to eat and the other men had gone to get some strong liquor.

"It's like a mausoleum only much more beautiful," Jaclyn agreed. She and Savannah had changed into their bathing suits and had already been into the pool several times. "I could stay here all day like this." She murmured. "Even though I don't know half these people."

"There are mostly friends of Caroline and some of them from the company." Jewel told her. She had started to feel the twinges again but she was determined not to ruin anyone's day by even mentioning it.

"Isn't your due date the fifth?" Savannah asked her.

"It is and I cannot wait." Jewel said with a sigh. "I feel as big as this place."

"Not even you could be as big as this place," Jaclyn told her with a laugh.

There were fireworks and food of all description and the party went on until way into the night. Her friends had left a little bit earlier saying they were going clubbing and they would be seeing her tomorrow. "Call us as soon as you feel the first contraction." Savannah told her, kissing her cheek as she got ready to leave.

"I will be sure to do that," Jewel told her with a smile.

*****

Jewel could not sleep. Jordan had finally drifted off at around one o'clock after making sure that she was not feeling any pains and that she was somewhat comfortable. The only way he had gone off to sleep was by her pretending that she was sleeping; but she was wide awake and the twinges had become more intense. She took deep breaths and eased herself up on the pillows, trying to stifle the moans coming from her throat. She wanted Jordan to sleep some more because she was sure this was not the real thing yet, they were too far apart.

She was still wide awake at two and the pain had started to come faster. It was when she let out a loud gasp that Jordan realized what was happening and jumped up. "Jews?" he mumbled sleepily reaching over to turn on the bedside lamp. Her face was tensed with pain and his heartbeat quickened. He was wide awake now! "How long?" his question was terse as he climbed off the bed.

"I started feeling it from this afternoon when the barbecue was going on," she admitted, breathing in and out.

"And you are just telling me now," He bit off an impatient sigh as he quickly pulled on the clothes he had worn yesterday.

"I am sorry, I just wanted to wait until it was time," She broke off as the pain bore down on her again.

He picked up his phone and called the doctor and then he called his mother and hers. They got to the bedroom when he was slipping a floral cotton dress over her head. "The contractions are now five minutes apart," he told them briefly. His hands trembled slightly as he smoothed down her hair. Her face was tensed with the pain and her hands were clenched into fists. He hated that she was going through this.

"Why don't you go get the car Jordan and we will finish getting her ready," Caroline suggested as she and Sylvia took charge.

"Yes go ahead honey, she will be okay, won't you sweetie?" Sylvia reached for a jacket and she slid her arms inside it.

Jewel nodded, meeting Jordan's eyes. He hesitated as if he could not bear to be away from her. "It's okay Jordan," He nodded and then left.

"Okay honey let's get you ready." Sylvia said briskly.

*****

Jordan drove with scant regards to the other drivers and barely paying attention to the traffic lights. His whole body tensed whenever she cried out during a contraction and he wished he could do something to make her stop feeling pain.

He arrived at the hospital in record time and the doctor was already there with a wheelchair and a nurse.

They wheeled her into the labor ward immediately and she was disrobed and changed into a green hospital gown.

"Okay Jewel," the doctor told her. "Do not push until I tell you to."

Jordan had been handed a robe as well and he sat by the edge of the bed holding her hand.

"I am right here baby," he told her softly. "I am not leaving."

Jewel nodded, feeling another contraction coming. She gasped and clung to Jordan's hand, her breath coming in a gasp that left her breathless and weak.

"The baby is crowning so I am going to ask you to push when you feel the contraction coming on." The doctor told her. "Jordan please go behind her and hold her upper body so that she can lean on you when she starts to push."

The contraction came with gigantic force this time and even though she had been given something for the pain, she still felt it radiating through her body. "Push!" the doctor instructed and she did, bearing back against Jordan as he held her hands. She rested back against him and he wiped her brow with a damp rag. "One more time Jewel and that's it."

She pushed with all her strength and fell back wearily against Jordan, a smile on her lips as she heard her daughter's angry wail. "Our daughter is here," Jordan said huskily still holding on to her.

*****

She slept as soon as they had cleaned her up and she held her daughter in her arms. She had brown curls and light green eyes, which the doctor said were probably going to change. She looked very much like her dad. He held her and stared down at the tiny figure in wonder. This was his daughter and he could not believe it. "I think she has your nose," he told her gently, as he sat beside her on the bed.

"Are you trying to make up for the fact that she has everything from you and nothing from her mother who carried her for nine months?" Jewel asked him amusement. She could barely remember the ordeal her body had been through just moments ago as she gazed at the exquisite picture her daughter and the man she loved made.
"Maybe," he grinned, bending forward to kiss her lips. "Thank you." He whispered.

So now she was asleep and Jordan had handed his daughter back to the nurse reluctantly. His mother and hers had exclaimed over the little beauty and had gone home to get some much needed sleep, but Jordan was not leaving. He had called Savannah and Jaclyn and they had come straight over to see the baby.

"She is a beauty isn't she?" Savannah stared at the little girl in fascination. She had already been tagged with her name: Jordanna Angela McIntyre as she watched a nurse adjust her blanket.

"She sure is," Jaclyn commented. They were both standing outside the nursery, staring in. "It kind of makes you want to have one."

"Not me. I am content to be Auntie Savannah for now." Savannah said firmly.

"I am going to want one very soon," Jaclyn said decisively.

"You are talking as if it's a house or a car that you are going to be purchasing," Savannah said dryly. "That's a living and breathing human being that you are going to be responsible for the next eighteen years or so."

"I am aware of that," Jaclyn told her. "That's why I am making sure that Tyler is the one first. I have no intention of being a single parent."

\*\*\*\*\*

She woke up to find them in her room and to the smell of jasmine and oleander and some kind of roses and lily, and of course a huge teddy bear.

"It's about time!" Jaclyn exclaimed, getting up from her position on one of the chairs and coming forward. "We thought you would never wake up."

Savannah came forward as well and they both sat on opposite sides of the bed. "So how does it feel to be a mommy?"

"It feels strange and scary at the same time." Jewel eased herself up against the pillows. She had no idea how long she had slept but right now she was famished. "Where did all these come from?" she asked in wonder.

"Some are from us and from Jordan's company and of course Caroline emptied out her greenhouse as well." Jaclyn told her with a grin. "I thought you were supposed to call us when you started to feel the first contraction."

"That of course was the farthest thing from my mind." Jewel said with a laugh. "Where is Jordan?"

"In the waiting room giving us a few minutes with you. Why don't you tell him to go home for a little bit? That man is exhausted." Savannah told her.

"I tried but he is not budging. I guess it has something to do with the fact that he was not here before. He is trying to make up for it."

"He sure is a keeper." Jaclyn said seriously.

"He is," Jewel agreed softly.

*****

"Are you sure you don't want to go home and get some sleep?" she lifted her head and looked at him. He was on the bed beside her and watched as she breastfed their daughter, fascinated by the little clenched fist on her mother's breast and the beautiful green eyes staring up at them.

"I am not leaving Jews," he said firmly, one hand reaching out to trace his daughter's fist. "I was not here before and I will never forget that, but this time I am here and I am not going anywhere."

"And I know that honey," she told him softly. "But I wished you would get some rest."

"I will rest later."

He sent out to get her take out and made sure that she ate before he left to get some coffee. He had called his office and told them that he was not going to be in for a few days and they should forward any important calls to him. He was not leaving her an inch. If that meant taking a shower in her bathroom then so be it. He had not been there when she had been pregnant the first time and he had not been there when she had lost their baby, so he was going to be around now.

He had stared at his daughter in fascination. He looked at her soft caramel complexion and her brown curls and the shape of her mouth and knew she was a McIntyre through and through. He had gone into the hospital chapel after she was safe and had sat on one of the benches and felt the tears coming down his cheeks. He was a father and his daughter was going to be looking to him for guidance and even though he could not be happier, he was also very scared. With all that was happening in the sick world that they lived in, how was he going to protect her from the evil that was out there?

He had a daughter! A little girl who was a tiny replica of him and he wanted to shout from the rooftop with happiness.

*****

She went home with her new born the next day after the doctor made sure that they were both okay. Her mother had come, as well as Caroline, Savannah and Jaclyn. who were following behind Jordan's vehicle.

He adjusted the mirror to make sure that she was all right before putting his eyes back on the road.

"You are going to be one of those fathers aren't you?" Jewel asked him in amusement.

"What father?" he glanced at her briefly, noticing with a sigh of relief that she looked very rested.

"The overprotective and unbearable father who thinks that no man is good enough for their daughter."

"No man will ever be good enough for her, I thought you knew that," he teased her, his green eyes laughing at her.

"Lord help anyone who looks at her cross eyed," Jewel said dryly reaching out to place a hand on his thigh, feeling the muscles flexed underneath her hand. "I am glad you were there the whole time."

"There was no place else I would have been," he clasped her hand tightly. "You are my two ladies and you are my family."

\*\*\*\*\*

"I cannot stop looking at her. Are all babies this perfect?" Jaclyn said to no one in particular. They had reached the house and Jordanna had settled inside her cot and was staring at all the faces around her.

"I am sure there are a few," Sylvia commented. "But my granddaughter of course takes the cake."

"How about giving her some room to breathe?" Caroline suggested. She had stood behind them feeling a little bit out of place. Even though she knew that both her son and Jewel had forgiven her for the past, she was still having a hard time forgiving herself.

They agreed with her and left the room, leaving only mother and father there. "They are right, she's beautiful isn't she?" Jewel said in an awed tone. She was standing beside the crib and Jordan was beside her with his arms around her.

"She sure is," he said with a smile.

*****

That night after her friends had left and both Caroline and Sylvia had retired for the night, Jordan sat in the nursery after telling Jewel to get some sleep. She had obeyed gratefully and after feeding her daughter had gone on to bed, feeling the exhaustion creeping up on her. He had his daughter in his arms rocking her and staring down at her when his mother came in. "Oh Jordan, I thought you had gone to bed." She said, getting ready to back out of the room.

"Come in mother," Jordan told her, indicating for her to take a seat beside him. The nursery had been decorated with elegant taste and the peach and cream décor was carried out in everything in the room, including the delicately made furniture.

It was a very large room and had several chairs there for people to sit on and a specially designed chair for when Jewel was breastfeeding or putting the baby to sleep. "Would you like to hold your granddaughter?"

"May I?" she asked in a humble voice, reaching for the baby.

"Of course." Jordan handed her the baby and saw the tears glistening in her eyes that were so like his.

"I cannot forgive myself for what I did to you and Jewel in the past and when I saw her and how beautiful she was, I felt regret go through me." She tore her gaze away from the baby and looked at her son. "I am so sorry Jordan. I wish that there was some way that I could make up for it."

"You are already making up for it mother." Jordan told her gently. "You are making amends and that's all I can ask for. I am sure you are going to be the best grandmother Angel will ever have, and that's enough."

"I am," she took the baby's hand and uncurled her little fist. "She looks so much like you that it's uncanny. She is a beautiful baby Jordan and you are going to be an excellent father."

"I certainly hope so," he stretched out his legs in front of him. "I have this sick feeling in the pit of my stomach, wondering if I am going to do something wrong; but above that, I know that I am going to be the father I am supposed to be to my daughter."

# Chapter 10

The dress was unbelievably beautiful! It had been flown in from Paris and was made of sheer chiffon and satin. It hugged her breasts and stomach and drifted gently down to her ankles in yards of material so light that it was like a cloud drifting around her. Her arms and shoulders were bare and she wore a sparkling diamond necklace that Jordan had given her as a wedding gift.

Their daughter was exactly two months old today and Jordanna cooed and looked curiously at the women in the room. She had been dressed already in a pink and white gown with a pink and white bow in her brown curls. Her eyes had darkened to the same shade of green as her father's and she was looking more and more like him every day.

"You certainly make a beautiful bride," Jaclyn said stepping back to look at her friend. They were going to be her bridesmaid and they were in gowns of a similar style but different colors. Jaclyn had on emerald green and Savannah was wearing aquamarine blue with matching flowers in their hair. Jewel was not wearing anything in her short cropped hair and her make-up was flawless. She pulled on the elbow length white gloves and lifted her dress. "I am ready." She said with a smile.

The wedding was being held outside on the lawn and even though it was the beginning of October, it was still warm enough to have the ceremony outdoors. The chairs had been set up and the gazebo had been decorated with white, green and aquamarine balloons and crepe papers and a huge bell at the center of the gazebo.

The sun was shining but was not hot enough to make the people already seated, uncomfortable.
Jaclyn went up first on the arm of Tyler, and then Savannah with Blake. The music changed, signaling to her that it was her turn.

Taking a deep breath she made her way up the aisle, vaguely aware that people were exclaiming over how she looked. She only had eyes for the man she had loved her entire life and their beautiful daughter in his arms. His hair was brushed back from his forehead and he looked so handsome in his dark blue tuxedo. He was looking at her with his intense green eyes.

He met her halfway, and shifting their daughter in his arms, he took her hand and placed it on his arm as they walked up together.

"I am inviting all of you to stand," the elderly minister said as soon as they reached him. "We are gathered together to witness the love between Jordan and Jewel. They will be saying their own vows."

Jordan handed his daughter to Jaclyn who was closest and turned to face Jewel, taking her hands. "Jewel, I have been given a second chance with you. I spent years thinking I had lost you and I was lost without you. I have loved you since we have been in high school and I thought that was intense, never dreaming that it could get more so," he smiled at her tenderly his hands tightening on hers. "I love you so much that I have to catch my breath each time I see you. You are the most beautiful woman I have ever seen and you will always be the only woman for me. You have given me a daughter and I am humbled by the fact that I will now be a husband as well as a father. I promise that I will treasure you, provide for you and never be unfaithful to you. I love you my darling, and always will."

"Jordan," Jewel began, her hands clinging to his. "You were my first and my only and you will always be it for me. I have no space for another man in my life because you have filled that space and I know that it will always be you. I love you my darling, my best friend, my lover, my everything and I promise that I will respect you and honor you all the days of my life."

There was a long silence as they stared at each other deeply. The minister cleared his throat and they turned towards him. "If there is anyone who objects to this union please speak now or forever hold your peace." He waited a spell then asked for the rings. "Please put the rings on," he instructed them. "Jordan Anthony McIntyre, will you take Jewel Marie Walsh to be your lawful wedded wife?"

"I do," he said clearly.

"Jewel Marie Walsh, will you take Jordan Anthony McIntyre to be your lawful wedded husband?"

"I do," she said with a small smile.

"By the power vested in me, I now pronounce you husband and wife. You may kiss your bride, sir." The minister said with a smile.

He clasped her cheeks with his hands and slowly bent his head to capture her lips with his in a slow passionate kiss that had them burning with passion.

"Ladies and gentlemen, I present to you, Mr. and Mrs. Jordan McIntyre".

There were sounds of applause as they walked down the aisle with Jordan holding his daughter in the crook of his arm and his wife on the other.

*****

"So how does it feel to be, not only a wife, but also a mother?" Jaclyn asked her. They were in her bedroom where they were helping her change out of the dress and put on a dazzling periwinkle blue gown which came to just above her knees. She had just fed Angel so the little girl was fast asleep in the nursery. After the reception they were going to be spending the night at the hotel uptown and both Caroline and Sylvia were going to be babysitting.

"It feels sensational." Jewel said with a laugh, looking at the pair of dazzling diamonds on her finger. "It also feels unreal. Four years ago I was trying to get my life back together after losing my child and thinking I had lost my man, and now I have been given a second chance. It feels out of this world."

They were all sitting on the bed and waiting while she put some things into an overnight bag. "You always had your man honey," Savannah said seriously. "That man never loved anybody but you and that is something that will never change as long as both of you are alive. I want what you have!" she said throwing up her hands in the air. "I heard what you said to each other and I cried. Honey, I have hope and as I said before, I will not settle. What you and Jordan have is something that is worth waiting for."

"I think I feel that way about Tyler," Jaclyn told them, settling back against the soft cotton sheets on the bed, her expression dreamy. "He is not Jordan but he is as close as one can get."

They heard a sound in the doorway and looked up to see Jordan standing there. "I am going to ask you to excuse us lady, but I am going to capture my wife now." He was not looking at them but had eyes only for her.

"Of course," Jaclyn slid off the bed and kissed Jewel on the cheek. "You have the real thing, don't ever forget that."

"Ready?" he entered the room. He had taken off his jacket and white shirt he had worn for the ceremony and had put on a light blue shirt.

"Right after we say goodbye to our daughter." She told him with a smile taking the hand he held out to her.

*****

He had reserved the honeymoon suite. It was a hotel that was owned by McIntyre and Company. They were treated like royalty the minute they arrived there.

"Mr. and Mrs. McIntyre, a pleasure to have you," the manager, a balding African American man with a slight paunch came forward to greet them and escorted them to the private elevator. "If there is anything you need, please do not hesitate to ask." He told them with a beaming smile as he stepped back from the elevator.

"Do you think we are going to need to call him?" Jordan asked her teasingly taking her into his arms.

"I strongly doubt it." Jewel looped her arms around his neck and raised her head to look at him. "I think I have everything I need right here."

"Absolutely," he murmured, bending his head to take her lips in a slow kiss that had her heart skidding inside her chest. She moved closer to him and returned the kiss with a fervor that had him bracing back against the cool chrome of the elevator wall. His erection poked inside his pants and he felt his heart thudding inside his chest. "My wife," he said with a groan and picking her up he swung her into his arms just as the door opened. He carried her all the way into the large suite only putting her down when they reached the middle of the room.

"It's beautiful," she breathed, her hands still on his arm as she stared around the bold black and red décor. She saw that there was a sitting room, a large bathroom and a balcony that faced the pool.

"You are beautiful," he tilted her chin to look at her. She was still wearing the earrings and the necklace he had given her and she looked so serenely beautiful that he could not stop looking at her. He had seen her walking up the aisle in the dress floating around her and he had had to blink to see if she was really real or just a vision thought up by his subconscious. She was real and she was his wife. "I keep expecting you to disappear into a cloud of smoke."

"I am not going to." She touched his strong jaw. "I love you my husband."

"Say it again," he whispered hoarsely.

"My husband." She repeated.

He lifted her up and strode with her to the bed where he put her down gently. There was a bottle of champagne chilling in the ice bucket beside the bed. He undressed her slowly and then himself, taking his time, his green eyes on hers. He removed the champagne from the bucket and took out a cube of ice and put it inside his mouth before joining her on the bed. It had been two months since they had been together that way and the anxiety was mounting up.

Jewel gasped as he took a nipple inside his mouth and the coldness of the ice cube met her pebble like nipple. He did the same to the other nipple and continued downwards slowly until he reached her pubic area. He touched her mound with it and by this time Jewel was almost out of her mind with need.

"Jordan," she cried out, her hands fisting into the soft sheets, her body on fire.

He removed the ice from his mouth and put it back on the table and returned to put his mouth there, his tongue snaking inside. Her body reared up as she felt the sensation racing through her body. "Please Jordan," she needed him inside her so badly that she could practically taste it.

He responded to her call and came over her, putting his erection into her tight opening. He was humbled by the fact that she had never been with anyone else but him and felt ashamed at the same time that he had been with a few women who had never meant anything to him. "I love you," she reached for him as he pushed further inside her. With a broken cry he covered her body with his, staying still to look at her, to savor the unbelievable sensation of being inside her that he had still not gotten accustomed to. This woman who had borne his daughter and now his name. The love he felt for her was so strong that it threatened to overwhelm him.

"I love you so much that I don't know if I can tell you," he whispered, his hands framing her exquisite face.

"Then show me," she told him softly, clasping him around the waist with her legs. He did, moving within her slowly at first then increasing the tempo as soon as she started moving. She had missed this! Oh how she had missed his penis inside her rubbing against the walls of her vagina and creating that sweet friction that make her want to spin out of control! She moved with him, clinging to him and brought his head down to meet her mouth. This was her man! Her husband and she could not quite believe that he was now truly hers. They belonged together because their souls met and joined as one, there was no parting them.

They came together their bodies tightening as the powerful orgasm flooded through them as if a flood gate had been opened! He swallowed her cries along with his hoarse ones and they rode the storm together!

Before they could even recover, he shifted position and placed her on top of him. She rested her head on his chest, loving the feel of his chest hair against her cheek as she closed her eyes and willed her heart to stop pounding so much.

Jordan held her against him closely, not willing to let her go. There was no need for words between them, they did not have to speak to be heard, they were so in tune with each other.

She drifted off to sleep eventually, her body on his. He did not go to sleep immediately, his brain was still too sharp and his body charged from the incredible sexual experience between them. She had so much control over his emotion that sometimes it scared him silly that this little slip of a girl held the key to his heart. He had always loved her, even when he had gone away and been with others, she had always intruded on his thoughts at the most inopportune times. He remembered being in a little village in Paris and he had thought he saw someone like her. He had hurried after her and realized that it was not her, and had been so bitterly disappointed that he had not been able to function for the rest of the week.

He hugged her to him and with a smile on his face he drifted off to sleep.

*****

They had breakfast brought up to them and he fed her strawberries covered with whipped cream. "I am surprised you did not call to find out if our daughter is okay," he told her teasingly.

"Who says I didn't?" she asked him loftily. "You were fast asleep when I woke up this morning. For your information our daughter woke up twice last night and was crying for her mother and father."

"She is okay?" he looked at her anxiously, ready to leave immediately.

"Now who is being the anxious parent?" she asked him mildly, rubbing whip cream on his nose.

"You are going to pay for that!" he growled.

"I am at your mercy," she told him huskily slipping off her pale silk robe and revealing her nakedness. "Show me how I can pay."

He did, abandoning the breakfast and pulling her into his arms. They did not leave the hotel room until way into the afternoon.

*****

Being married to Jordan was far different from living with him. He made her aware that she was his wife ever single chance he got. He showered her with gifts of clothing, jewelry until she started protesting that she was going to give away some of them if he did not stop! He made her feel so special that Jewel wondered if she was living a fairy tale.

Maude had offered to look after Jordanna when Jewel reluctantly went back to work. Her mother had finally flown back to Florida promising that she would be back before they knew it. "I don't want my granddaughter to grow up without me." She had said as she kissed the soft cheek of the baby who stared up at her and made cooing sounds.

"I cannot believe you are engaged!" Jewel exclaimed. Her friends had come by for a visit. It was the first Saturday in November and the time had gotten decidedly chilly. Jordan had made himself scarce and had run into the office for a few hours. Jewel had stopped working on Saturdays in order to spend more time with her daughter who was growing in leaps and bounds.

"It's not the rock that Jordan gave you but I love it," Jaclyn said holding her hand out with the solitaire diamond winking on her finger. "He was so romantic and he went down on one knee in front of the entire restaurant where we were having dinner and proposed. I cried!"

"I would have loved to see that," Savannah said dryly. "How the mighty have fallen."

Jaclyn took a cushion from the sofa and threw it at her.

"Girls please! No violence in the nursery." Jewel said with a laugh rubbing Angel's back so she could burp. She had just breastfed her and Caroline was coming to get her so that she and her friends could celebrate Jaclyn's engagement.

"Hi girls," Caroline breezed in just then, her blonde hair in a ponytail and her tall lithe body clad in denims and a red cashmere sweater. "Ah, there is my girl. All fed and pretty in pink." She took the baby from her daughter in law and inhaled her baby smell.

"Where are you two off to?" Jaclyn asked her

"We are going for a ride in the country and then shopping." Caroline looked at Jewel. "I know but I saw the cutest little outfit in my favorite baby store and I have to get it for her."

"You said that several days ago when you bought those dresses for her," Jewel reminded her dryly.

"I can't help it, she is so adorable." Caroline picked up the baby bag and got ready to leave. "We will see you later."

"She sure has changed." Savannah commented as soon as she left.

"We are getting along so well that I find myself wondering if this is the same woman who made my life a living hell all those years ago." Jewel said with a shake of her head. She stood up to put away the things she had used to get her daughter ready. "Girls, I love being a wife and a mother and in spite of what Jordan says I am going to have another child."

"You are going to wait just a little bit though?" Jaclyn said as they made their way to the kitchen. It was almost lunch time and Jewel had had Stefan send something up for them to eat.

"Of course I am!" Jewel said with a smile. "Angel does not need the competition right now."

"Good." Savannah told her climbing on one of the stools and reaching for one of the tiny sandwiches there. "From the way you sound just now it would seem that you are ready to get pregnant right now."

"When is the wedding?" Jewel turned back the conversation to her friend who was foraging inside the fridge to find something to drink.

"We are planning a Christmas wedding, but it might be February, we are not sure yet." Jaclyn placed a bottle of non alcoholic wine on the counter and settled on the stool. She had also brought wine glasses to pour the wine into. "Let's make a toast to men who can hear the word commitment and actually not run a mile away."

"That's one way to put it." Savannah said with a grin lifting her glass.

"To men who are real men." Jewel said softly, lifting her glass in a toast.

*****

"Do you think we are going to be like this when we are old and gray and our sex drive has gone through the window?" Jewel asked as her husband rubbed the special cream over her stomach and thighs. She had been using it during her pregnancy and continued to use it because it made her skin feel silky soft.

Their daughter had been put down for the night after spending a hectic day with her grandmother who had come back with numerous amounts of shopping bags. "We had a whale of a time," she had said with a grin.

"Of course not," Jordan responded rubbing the cream into her inner thighs, his hands kneading the muscles of her leg. They had taken a shower together and both of them were completely naked. "We are going to sit on the balcony on rocking chairs designed for that purpose and we are going to hold hands and look at the sunset."

"You make it sound so romantic." Jewel teased, her brown eyes meeting his green ones.

"It is," He murmured, his hand inching further inside her legs towards her pubic area. "Open up for me." He instructed her.

"You didn't have to ask," she told him huskily as she opened her legs wider. "It's yours for the taking."

"Glad to hear that," his fingers touched her there as he rubbed some of the cream on her mound. "Our love will only grow stronger." He added as he climbed on top of her and entered her slowly. "No doubt about that."

The end.

If you enjoyed this ebook and want me to keep writing more, please leave a review of it on the store where you bought it. By doing so you'll allow me more time to write these books for you as they'll get more exposure. So thank you. :)

## Get Free Romance eBooks!

Hi there. As a special thank you for buying this book, for a limited time I want to send you some great ebooks completely **free of charge** directly to your email! You can get it by going to this page:

## www.saucyromancebooks.com/physical

You can see a the cover of these books on the next page:

ONE LONE COWBOY, ONE WOMAN ON A MISSION...

# THE LONE COWBOY

EMILY J

ROCHELLE

RE MET HIS MATCH?

UCH ASS

LDING

IF IT'S MEANT TO BE...

*Him*

KIMBERLY GREENFORD

PLAYERS GONNA PLAY?

SHE'S THE ONE HE WANTS
BUT CAN SHE TRUST HIM?

ONE VAMPIRE. ONE COP. ONE LOVE.

# VAMPIRES OF CLEARVIEW

J A FIELDING

**These ebooks are so exclusive you can't even buy them.**
When you download them I'll also send you updates when
new books like this are available.

Again, that link is:

## www.saucyromancebooks.com/physical

Now, if you enjoyed the book you just read, please leave a
positive review of it where you bought it (e.g. Amazon). It'll
help get it out there a lot more and mean I can continue writing
these books for you. So thank you. :)

## More Books By Mary Peart

If you enjoyed that, you'll love Her Russian Billionaire's Baby
by Cher Etan (sample and description of what it's about below
- search 'Her Russian Billionaire's Baby by Cher Etan' on
Amazon to get it now).

## Description:

Adrian is from a very... Russian family.

He's also a billionaire, and can have pretty much whatever he wants.

Isobel on the other hand runs a quaint pastry shop, has money problems and is pretty much his opposite in every way.

But when a chance and rather awkward meeting between the two occurs, both of their lives will be changed forever!

What does true love with a handsome Russian feel like?

Like your world's complete, like you want his baby, like you want to marry him.

But what about when his dark and dangerous mafia ties starts to show and you get caught in the middle of it all?

Will they be able to overcome hurdles that involve not only themselves, but also the mob?

Want to read more? Then search 'Her Russian Billionaire's Baby Cher Etan' on Amazon to get it now.

Also available: One Billionaire Cowboy, One Baby by Steffy Shaw (search 'One Billionaire Cowboy, One Baby Steffy Shaw' on Amazon to get it now).

## Description:

When vet Naomi Kaye gets a job on a local farm, she expects it to be just another 'day at the office'.

What she finds instead is a ranch run by Jack, a handsome and very, very rich cowboy.

Jack recently sold his business for a lot of money in order to concentrate on his passion: farming full time.

The only thing missing in his life?

A loyal and caring woman to share his down time with.

Will Naomi be that caring and hard working soul he's looking for?

And when she gets pregnant with Jack's child, will they be able to overcome the forces trying to split the two apart?

Want to read more? Then search 'One Billionaire Cowboy, One Baby Steffy Shaw' on Amazon to get it now.

You can also see other related books by myself and other top romance authors at:

**www.saucyromancebooks.com/romancebooks**

50879043R00106

Made in the USA
Lexington, KY
03 April 2016